STONE COLD

A STONE COLD THRILLER

J. D. WESTON

STONE COLD

CHAPTER ONE

Two men slipped silently through the door of warehouse twenty-four. It was a generic warehouse building, typically found in business parks all over the world. This particular unit was in Beckton, East London, and the park was aptly named 'The East London Business Park.' Harvey Stone closed the door behind them, careful to make no sound. He turned to his companion, Julios, and nodded. The movement was barely discernible in the pitch darkness, but Julios understood the signal and moved forward, listening for any change in noise from the room beyond.

They had entered through a narrow door that opened into a small hallway. Stairs on their right led up to a row of mezzanine offices, and a door directly in front of them led out to the large warehouse space, where several men could be heard loading a truck. They listened to the whirr of a heavy battery-powered forklift and the hiss of hydraulic rams lowering its cargo onto the truck. The sounds were clear in the otherwise silent warehouse.

Julios chanced a glance through the gap in the semi-open connecting door. He watched intently for a while before holding three fat fingers up to Harvey, who stood behind him in the darkness, still and alert.

The three men in the warehouse worked in silence. There was no banter and no casual insults to pass the time. There was no sound at all save for the whirrs, hisses and metallic rattles of the machinery.

Julios and Harvey had a plan they would carry out precisely. It was the only way to ensure a one-hundred percent chance of success. According to Julios' tried and tested methodology, deviation from any plan caused variants in possibilities. Julios did not like variants. They led to mistakes, and in their line of work, mistakes often ended in death.

Harvey and Julios heard the sliding tailgate of the truck followed by the light, metallic click of a padlock. As the diesel engine fired up, then came the twin thumps of the closing truck doors, which boomed around the large warehouse. The screeching of the sliding concertina shutters began their banshee-like cry as they were pulled open to allow the truck to leave. Once it had pulled out and the sound of its engine had faded away, the sliding shutter was closed with a crash. Chains were dragged through a series of steel rings then padlocked, marking the end of the audible warehouse performance.

Every detail played out in Harvey's mind. A lifetime of working in the dark had tuned his senses to noise, allowing him to visualise minute details. He and Julios remained in the shadows, blocking the one remaining exit for the one remaining man. There had been three men in the warehouse, and two truck doors had been slammed, which left only one. Exactly as they had planned.

Julios moved further into the blackness, ready for the door to open, and gave a silent signal for Harvey to follow suit. They waited in practised silence, listening to sounds and imagining their meanings.

A new noise. Four digital clicks of a smartphone being unlocked followed by a stutter of taps, indicating a message being sent. Then the warehouse lights turned off. There were six switches in two rows of three, according to Harvey's interpretation of the timing of each click. Total darkness ensued. But Julios didn't need light to carry out the job.

A familiar lift in Harvey's heart rate sent a thrilling warmth through his body. His eyes pulsed once as the adrenaline released and he rolled his neck from side to side, waiting for the two satisfying clicks.

He was ready.

The sound of footsteps and jangling keys grew closer until, at last, the little door creaked open and their target stepped into the trap. The man hadn't taken two steps into the hallway when Julios' huge black shape emerged from the darkness and slipped a steel wire around his neck.

As Julios had instructed, Harvey remained where he was, watching with awe at the panicked struggle in the darkness. The only sounds were a few feeble squeals of the man's trainers skidding on the painted concrete floor and the sickly, choking sound of his few last breaths.

Julios was a pro. Harvey admired his control and composure during these moments and looked on with admiration. Emotion was not a factor in the transaction. No anger, spite, or bitterness tainted his methods. He was, in Harvey's eyes, a master of his trade.

Their instructions had been simple. *Leave no clues. Make a statement.*

Julios waited his standard one minute after the moment he believed his work to be done. The one-minute rule applied to nearly every aspect of the job. Above all else, it added an element of control when instinct might favour haste.

Julios' gloved fingers tugged at the wire trace then pocketed the weapon.

Leave no clues.

He looked up at Harvey, who was waiting in the shadows on the second step of the staircase and nodded at him in the darkness, signifying that it was Harvey's turn to perform.

Make a statement.

Harvey stepped over the body and, using a small, two-cell torch, found the light switches on the wall of the warehouse. Two rows of three, exactly as he had guessed. He used the point of his knife to turn on just one switch then pocketed the torch. The knife-point wouldn't rub off any existing finger-prints and certainly wouldn't leave his own.

He glanced at the front end of the ware-house. There was an electric chain hoist on a running beam fixed to a series of overhead gantries roughly ten metres high. The run-ning beam led from above the large shutters all the way to the rear of the warehouse where the mezzanine floor stored large machinery and crates. Presumably, the hoist was used for loading and unloading flatbed lorries.

But Harvey had another use for it in mind.

A yellow console with two buttons marked with up and down arrows hung from the hoist by a thick cable. Harvey hit the down button and the hoist jumped into life, lowering a large hook on the end of its chain. He waited for it to reach knee level then re-leased the button.

The dead man's body slid across the painted concrete floor with little effort. As Harvey dropped him beside the hook, he saw an angry red line across the man's throat.

Beside the doors, Harvey found a broom that he smashed against the wall until he was left with just the handle. He slid it through the dead man's jacket sleeves then wrapped the chain around his limp body before connecting it to the large hook. The hoist jumped into life once more and, inch by inch, the man rose into the air with his head rolled forwards and his lifeless body hanging in the shape of the cross.

Harvey stopped the hoist when the hook reached its maximum height and stepped back to admire his work. Ten metres high and a picture of perfection, their target stared back at Harvey and Julios.

An ill-feeling crawled across Harvey's skin, unfamiliar and tense. He stared back at the statement he'd been told to make and knew in the deepest, darkest pit of his gut that they'd crossed the line.

He and Julios had just started a war.

CHAPTER TWO

Driving in silence afforded Frank Carver a rare opportunity to think clearly without the background noise and interruptions of office life. He drove at a slow but steady sixty miles an hour on the M25 motorway and prepared to take the next exit, which would lead him onto the M11 then subsequently onto the North Circular Road and into Beckton. It was late morning, so the roads were clearer than during the rush hour madness.

One of the cases he'd been working on was building up. He had a feeling it was all going to come crashing down soon enough, and in his experience, he would need to be there when it did. He'd need to ensure the rewards came his way and the right suspects were locked up.

If he left it to anyone else, the lead investigator would settle for prosecuting anybody involved, but with no hard strategy. To nail a big fish, you needed a strategy, an infallible plan that produced irrefutable evidence. Anything less and big fish would sink below the surface of their legitimate operations for a few years until it's all blown over and their smart lawyers found a loophole. Only then would they commit themselves to another big job. By then, Frank planned on being retired.

Frank wouldn't let Terry Thomson slip away this time, and he'd take down anyone who stood in his way.

Frank had been informed of a body found inside a warehouse of an East London business park. One of his team had designed a computer tool to sniff for tags in the Metropolitan Police database. It had flagged the case as soon as it was logged. The warehouse was leased by an affiliate company of Thomson.

In the old days, links between cases and new information were easily missed, and he'd likely never have heard about it. But these days, not a lot was missed. In fact, too many leads were generated, of which only a handful were useful. The trick was to sift through the pile and identify the ones that *would* lead somewhere.

He took the next exit and followed the slip road onto the dreaded A13, the main artery into London from the east, which was notorious for its heavy congestion. Then he turned off into Beckton and drove slowly down the road to the business park, which was bumpy from years of fully laden lorries driving in and out.

At the far end, he could see the spinning lights of the local police. Frank switched off the sat-nav and rolled to a stop beside a bored-looking policeman, who stood by two traffic cones and a roadblock. He hit the button to lower the passenger window.

"You'll have to turn around, sir," said the officer with a Manchester twang. "The road is closed for the morning, I'm afraid."

Frank flashed his ID before the officer could finish and continued to drive forwards, squeezing his Volvo through the small gap between the police car and the traffic cone. Outside the warehouse, he parked between a forensics van and an ambulance. Inside, he pulled on a pair of blue shoe protectors and ducked beneath the red and white tape, flashing his ID once more to an officer guarding the single door.

In Frank's mind, a murder scene broke down into stages: the entry, the act, and the exit.

The warehouse doors showed no sign of forced entry, suggesting they were left un-locked or the killer was invited inside. The kill was clean with no sign of struggle, but the killer had gone to great lengths to humiliate the victim, which suggested that time was not an issue. Due to the location, the exit would've been made using a vehicle.

A mark across the victim's throat identi-fied the probable cause of death as strangula-tion, garrotting, to be precise. Given the immaculate crime scene and lack of evidence, Frank knew the weapon was taken by the murderer. But when Frank pulled on a pair of synthetic gloves and used the bright yellow console to lower the hook, the case became truly interesting. Inside the victim's jacket, he found a smartphone and a brown leather wal-let, which held a few hundred pounds in twenty-pound notes, three credit cards and a driving license.

The name on the front of the license was Bradley Thomson.

If two and two equalled four, the white-faced and stone-cold body that hung from the hook like a centrepiece in a museum was the son of the renowned East End villain, Terry Thomson. The very man he wanted to put away.

Pieces of a hazy puzzle fell into place in Frank's mind. Bradley had been garrotted with zero mess. There was no blood and no damage to the immediate environment. This all suggested that the killer was old school and a pro. These days, killers had no style. Too many Hollywood films made dealing with a messy murder an all-too-frequent part of the job. But a messy murder leaves clues. Bradley Thomson's killer left no trace.

Hanging Bradley's body was either a message or a statement. Either way, the murder was suicidal. The killer would need an army to stop Terry Thomson's retaliation, and despite Thomson's numerous enemies, there weren't many people who had that amount of manpower.

It wasn't often that Frank saw the work of a pro anymore. Not in a murder anyway. He hadn't officially worked a straight murder case for years. He missed the challenge. He'd enjoyed his work back then, but it hadn't left much room for talk over dinner. Instead, he would listen to his wife rattle on about the neighbour's dog or the local shop being bought out. Yet, given the chance, he would give everything to hear Jan rattle on one more time.

Forensics were hunting for fingerprints on the surrounding environment and footprints in the dust. They spoke of having the body checked for third-party DNA. The local investigators were following a standard procedural template, which rarely left room for common sense and creativity. It was more like data collection. Later, somebody lower in the ranks would feed the information into a computer and hope for it to spit out the right answer. It rarely did.

Frank thought it was pointless to hunt for clues on the scene when the killer had clearly been carrying out a job for someone else. Time could be more efficiently spent hunting the man who gave the order or checking the surrounding areas where the perpetrator may have been less diligent about leaving traces of evidence. Pros like this were hired men.

Using his phone, Frank took a photo of the abrasions on Bradley Thomson's neck and face before heading back outside. He'd been inside the warehouse for less than ten minutes. He walked past two women who were standing nearby, both stifling tears. It was cold out and they hugged each other for warmth and comfort.

"Excuse me, ladies," said Frank. "Did either of you know the victim?"

The elder of the two women dropped her face into her hands and whined. The other offered Frank a stern look and pulled her friend closer.

"We both did," she said. "We found him this morning. Who would do something like this?"

"That's what we're going to find out. Have you both given a statement?"

The woman nodded.

"Good," said Frank. "Don't worry. We'll catch them."

He left the women and moved along the row of warehouses. Cameras were fixed to tall poles at the entrance. Another was fixed to the side of the building and pointing down the road at oncoming traffic. But no cameras were facing into the park. It was as if the security designer had deemed it unnecessary because all traffic had to come in through the gates.

Frank continued his walk along the front of the neighbouring units, many of which had people standing outside them in the cold, trying to get a look at the commotion. He wore jeans and a loose-fitting button-up shirt under a long jacket that hid the paunch he'd been developing for the past few years. Onlookers turned and watched him walk by, but he didn't look back.

At the far end of the units was a small copse of trees with a steel fence marking the perimeter of the business park. It had two-inch steel bars running vertically every four inches. A person might get their hands between the rails but not much else, and the sharp, angled tops of each bar would certainly prevent anybody from climbing over.

But at the end of the fence, closest to the warehouses, Frank found a gap. Two bent steel bars had been forced off, probably with a car jack, and were laid on the grass outside the perimeter.

There were no footprints to disturb, so he stepped through the hole, careful not to rip his jacket. Then he walked among the trees until he found himself at the dual carriageway which ran behind the estate and up to the North Circular Road.

He'd found the exit.

The section of road was fast-moving by day as it bypassed the A13. But at night, Frank knew it would be empty save for the odd taxi or night-worker. It would give the killer ample opportunity to get away unseen.

A single tyre track was barely visible in the long grass, but at the right angle and in the right light, it was clear as day. Frank looked closer. He traced the faint path and found a small patch of mud between two clumps of grass.

He smiled to himself.

Got you.

The print wasn't very clear but clear enough for Frank to take a photo. He lay a ten-pound note on the ground and snapped a shot. The ten-pound note would provide accurate scaling for Tenant, his tech research guy, to identify the tyre tracks.

Returning to the investigation with a positive sense of accomplishment, Frank found the inspector in charge, who was requesting camera footage from a security guard. The guard wore an ill-fitting, bright yellow, high-visibility jacket and, judging by the way he was shrugging, was of little use.

"A word in your ear," said Frank in his soft Scottish accent. "Those cameras won't show anything. That's a waste of time." He turned and nodded towards the fence. "He came from that way. There's a gap in the railings and a motorbike track in the dirt. You can dust the fence for prints. You won't find any, but send me the results of the track analysis as soon as you have them. I'll need a list of motorbikes that tyre might belong to." He handed the bemused inspector his card. "I'll be waiting for your email."

Frank stepped away from the scene. He hadn't mentioned that he'd already identified the victim and knew the significance of the murder; the investigator could waste precious time figuring that out. Frank would be well ahead by that time. Besides, as Bradley was heir to the Thomson throne, as it were, the case would land on Frank's lap anyway. His team of organised crime specialists were far more likely to get to the bottom of it.

He returned to the warmth of his car and sent the photos to his small team. He glanced back at the hive of activity, knowing that the uniforms would glean less from the crime scene in an entire day than Frank had in less than half an hour.

CHAPTER THREE

Sergio woke early, as he did each morning, to the soprano melody of Strauss' Epheu. The crisp tones from the inbuilt ceiling speakers flowed throughout his small but lavish apartment one mile from John Cartwright's estate in the village of Theydon Bois in Essex. The hardwood floors gave resonance to the sound. Sergio smiled at the dexterity of the vocalist and slid from the smooth, black, silk sheets into the cold bite of the air-conditioning.

He glanced back at the girl who had stayed overnight. She slept naked and quietly. Her mouth was open just a fraction, showing the tips of her perfect young teeth beneath her full lips. The smooth sheets lay across her body and her arm was exposed, revealing one soft and firm breast. Her nipple stood proud and hard, exposed to the cool air that circulated the apartment. Sergio checked his email and messages on his phone then took a sly video of the sleeping girl. He hardened at the thought of watching it later that evening when she had left. He would add it to his collection.

He showered in the tiled, black, en-suite bathroom and dressed in a black tailored shirt and suit. Saville Row's finest. His shirt was ring-spun and smooth to the touch like silk. But the material retained a masculine look with its matte finish, unlike Italian materials, which, in Sergio's opinion, were cheap-looking.

For breakfast, he ate yoghurt with banana and drank fresh coffee made with Ethiopian beans direct from the source. He placed his dish, cup and spoon in the dishwasher. The maid would turn it on and empty it when she arrived later. He saw an upturned martini glass from the previous night. It was tainted with the lipstick of the sleeping girl, and he remembered her lips fondly.

His mornings were clockwork. Disruption

to his patterns caused disruptions to his thinking, which led to mistakes. And John would not tolerate mistakes. Sergio walked across to the bedroom and woke the girl by cupping the breast that was offered in the cool air. She breathed in deeply and murmured in a sleepy voice. He squeezed a little harder until she gasped.

"Does daddy want to play some more already?" The girl smiled and opened her eyes. Seeing Sergio fully dressed, she said, "Oh, so early. You have to leave?"

"It's *you* that has to leave, I'm afraid," he replied coldly.

She ran her hand up his leg and found what she was looking for growing in excitement as she returned the squeeze.

"Are you sure you can't stay a little longer?" she asked, finding the zipper and giving it a soft tug.

He considered the thought of being ten minutes late. He was technically an hour *early* each day anyway, so a ten-minute delay would not actually result in him being *late*. The girl reached inside and gripped him between finger and thumb. Her gaze followed his body up to his eyes as she moved her mouth closer to him and ran her hands across the smooth material of his shirt.

Desire overcame his rigid professionalism, and he let her touch him. He enjoyed toying with women. He enjoyed the power, the power to say no, the power to stop them when he commanded. To be the boss for once. He enjoyed the girl a moment longer, then pulled away.

"Now get up. You're leaving."

She sat back on the bed and looked at him incredulously. "Is that how you treat such a nice gesture?"

"Are you dressing?" he asked, as he paced around the bed. "In one minute, you are leaving this apartment, dressed or not."

He left and heard the pillow bounce softly across the room behind him.

"Pig!"

The view from the kitchen looked out over Epping Forest. Sergio enjoyed watching the trees sway gently in the breeze. Birds flew from one branch to another in a restless state of fear and hunger, just like workers in the city.

The front door slammed as the girl left

and Sergio smiled to himself. She had been expensive, but worth every penny.

His Mercedes waited for him in the small basement car park of the apartment building. It seemed to wake like a happy puppy with a push of the key fob. The headlights and indicators flashed on then dimmed, the locks popped open, and the soft inner light gently brightened the plush leather interior.

The expensive car stereo picked up from where the apartment stereo had left off and continued with the delights of Strauss as the large saloon pulled out of the car park and onto the back streets of Theydon Bois. Sergio turned up the volume as he drove past the hooker, ignoring her gesture, and headed towards the office to hear the news from Julios and Harvey.

Sergio's day had started well.

CHAPTER FOUR

Only the wind whistling through the windows and the tapping fingers of the old oak tree against the misted glass accompanied the bright flashes of lightning that lit the boy's room long enough to set his wild imagination spiralling. Dark shadows of friendly toys teased his fear with their large, crooked noses, pointed chins and long, gnarled fingers. The black spaces between objects grew deeper and darker with each crack of thunder. With the bed sheets pulled up to his eyes, he waited for dawn, when daylight would banish the shadows and the songs of birds would ward off the wind.

He began to hum a tune his foster father

often played on his record player. The melody began with the high and innocent cry of a scared and lonely violin as if it walked unaccompanied through a deep forest. Slowly, the orchestra grew, as if strangers stepped from behind the trees to face the darkness together. The strength and confidence of the violin grew with each additional sound and the dark shadows faded with each instrumental entrance. The volume rose to an almighty high to break through the canopy of trees and let the sunlight shine down to guide the way of the orchestra. The tempo, chaotic yet rhythmic, fought the resilient darkness whose desperate talons clung to the fat trunks of gnarled trees. Then the beating heart of a timpani, strong and bold, fell in line, bringing up the rear, pumping life into the ensemble, and casting the deathly shadows back to where they belonged.

And then there was light.

A single violin sang its soulful tune, confident and unafraid.

The sheets slipped from the boy's face and cold air breathed across his skin. Hard patters of rain washed against the glass outside in waves, blown this way and that by the incessant wind. He rose from his bed, placed his bare feet on the cold, wooden floor and crept to the window, driven by wonder and hoping to see the tail of the banished storm.

But the storm lingered, waiting in the dark clouds high in the sky. Its tenacious claws gripped the old oak and at the peak of the wind, when the wash of rain threatened to break through the glass, it crashed its fist down with an angry crack of thunder. Lightning flashed in a series of strikes and the wind tore a huge branch from the old oak, which fell against the house, grinding and scratching its way to the dark ground.

The small boy turned and saw the foreboding shapes of his toys against the cold, hard wall, which seemed to rise above his own cowering shadow. He ran from the room and into the corridor, slipping on the wood until he crashed into his sister's room. Slamming the door, he leaned breathlessly against the wood as the wind circled the house, carrying with it a perpetual stream of leaves and rain.

He slipped into his sister's bed, shaking with fear but safe in her presence. They were together, and together, they could face anything. He lay with his back to her back and placed the soles of his cold, young feet against the warmth of hers. The anger of the storm faded away into the night.

He dreamed they were running along a beach through the long, wild grass that bordered golden sand, laughing and rolling, and staring up at the sky, making shapes from its wispy formations. But then there were none. Grey sky pushed away the blue. White clouds grew darker like a cancer working its way through the shape and blackening its heart. The light was banished, unable to penetrate the evil gloom.

The boy woke with a start.

His feet searched for his sister's but found nothing.

He rolled and padded the bed, but she was gone. He was alone. There was only a warm patch where she had been laying and a hollow in the pillow. Once more, the cold floor nipped his feet as he padded across the room and opened the door a crack. The house was still. The invading storm had moved on, leaving a trail of destruction and fear.

He crept along the corridor to the great hallway where two grand staircases curved then met on the ground floor like evil arms welcoming guests into their lair. Keeping to the edge of the stairs to avoid the creaks and groans of the wood, he passed the oil paintings whose dull and unsmiling faces stared at him with contempt until he reached the hard, wooden floor below.

There was a sound. A murmur. It was shrill and out of place alongside the subtle moans of the old house.

He stepped through to the kitchen behind the stairs where the hard terracotta tiles bit his skin. Resting one foot on top of the other, he switched when the pain was too much, all the time, listening. The room ran across the width of the building with windows along its length that flooded the space with bright moonlight. It shone across the kitchen surfaces, licked at the sides of the old pots and pans that hung from the exposed beams, and lit the round, brass handle of the small cellar door.

That sound again. A rhythmic groan of pain and tears.

His hand, shaking with terror, reached for the brass handle which seemed to beg to be touched, shining bright against the dark wood.

But there were footsteps on the stairs below, heavy boots and the cough of a man un-afraid of the night, unafraid of anything.

The boy sank into the shadows. He backed into the dark space beneath the kitchen surface, amongst sacks of potatoes and protected by the very shadows that had tormented him all night.

The cellar door opened with the creak of old wood, revealing the sound of that rhythmic grunting, tears, and agony, loud in the night. It was all wrong. So wrong. From the doorway emerged a man, tall, lean and gaunt, who stepped into the kitchen. Closing the door behind him, nothing more than a distant whisper was left of the pain below and the mournful sobs lost to the night.

Then came the metallic click of a cigarette lighter and the man's deep inhale of smoke. He rolled his head back and sighed with pleasure then allowed a soft, breathless release of poisoned air. From where the boy hid, he could see through the window beyond. The bright moon framed a large, crooked nose, a deep, pointed chin and the outline of a face that would change his life forever.

CHAPTER FIVE

Frank's phone rang over the car's Bluetooth system.

"Carver."

"Sir, we received your photos," said Melody Mills, his lead investigator. "You're on loudspeaker with me, Tenant and Cox. Did you find anything useful?"

"Did you see the victim?" asked Frank.

"We did, sir. Not sure what to think of that."

"Things are about to get messy, Mills," replied Frank. "Are you able to identify the bike from the picture of the tyre track?"

"I can try, sir," said Reg Tenant. "I can get

a list of bikes that might fit the bill. It'd give us a starting point."

"Good. Can we have it ready by the time I get back to the office?"

"I'm on it now, sir."

"Mills?"

"Sir?"

"Research. We need eyes and ears out there. There's a change in the air. I want to know which way the wind's blowing."

"I'll see what I can find, sir. Did the job look pro?"

"Clean as a baby's arse, Mills."

"Looked like a garrotting from the photos. Am I right?" asked Mills.

"Spot on. Neat job. Would have been over in seconds."

"We'll pull up all the garrottings then. Maybe there's a link in the method."

"Good. We need to know what the Thomsons are involved in right now, and what they're planning. Whoever did this is either stupid or has some serious balls."

"There are only two real main players, sir, the Stimsons and the Cartwrights," said Melody. "Killing is not Stimson's style, but let's not write him off."

"Agreed," said Frank. "But for John Cartwright to have a go at Thomson would be like poking a sleeping bear."

"You would need a big stick to poke that bear, sir."

"You would. Even then, you'd be asking for trouble. See what sticks Cartwright has in his arsenal. See if there's one big enough to take out Bradley Thomson."

"Will do, sir."

"Oh, and Mills?"

"Sir?"

"Have Cox sort out that van. I can see this going mobile," said Frank. "Find out where Thomson is holed up these days and plan for a recce."

"I'm right here, sir," said Cox.

Denver Cox wasn't an investigator or a tech research guru. He was an engineer assigned to the unit, and he came with a certain set of skills that had come in handy on numerous occasions. Denver was a first-class rally driver trained by the best. He'd also obtained his private pilot's license and CAA-approved helicopter license, which gave him a leg up over other drivers and engineers. It also meant that Frank rarely let him get seconded to other units. There had been a few times when Frank had to step in and block a request for Denver's time, much to the annoyance of other lead investigators.

"Good," said Frank. "We need that van up and running. You're going to be busy over the next few days, and we can't have it just sitting on the side of a road somewhere."

"The van is golden, sir," said Denver. "It won't be an issue."

"Good stuff."

"And Stimson, sir?" asked Mills. "Do you want me to bother with him? Or do you want me to concentrate on Cartwright? You know, the process of elimination."

"The mythological Stimson? See what you can find. But don't hold your breath. I haven't laid eyes on him in the thirty years I've been on the job. Chances are you'll find people that work for him, but they'll have their mouths bound shut with fifty-pound notes. Anyway, you won't get any further than that. Better to find our killer. Find him and he'll lead us right into the hornets' nest."

CHAPTER SIX

Terry Thomson spoke quietly and slowly but never once raised his eyes from the framed photo on his desk.

"Why wasn't I told sooner?"

"We've only just found out, boss," said Lenny. "Apparently, the police took his..." He stopped and adjusted his sentence. "Took *him* away for examining. They didn't release the news until they had to officially."

"How?" asked Terry.

It was a question Lenny had been both expecting and dreading.

"Strangled, boss," he began. Lenny spoke with no fear or hesitation. He gave it to Terry straight. "Steel wire around his neck. It would have been quick."

Terry nodded and pondered on how his son might have looked in that moment. Then he wondered why he hadn't fought back. It wasn't as if Bradley was a pushover. He could look after himself.

"Was it a professional, Lenny?" asked Terry.

"It looks like it. No prints. No sign of anyone. No evidence."

"Who found him? Who else knows?"

"The woman who opens the yard saw him when she walked in. He was hanging from the hoist by a chain. So all the girls at the yard know. They've been told not to shout about it. Police closed the scene off pretty quick so no-one else got a look in."

"Any ideas about who it might be?"

"None, boss," replied Lenny. "Do you want me to put the feelers out?"

Terry nodded. "If you find him, Lenny, I want him alive. Make sure the boys know that this one is mine." He paused and fought to control his wavering voice. "Thanks, Lenny. Can you give me a bit? I need some time alone."

CHAPTER SEVEN

For Harvey, the drive to John Cartwright's office in nearby Chigwell was mostly country lanes free of traffic. John was originally from neither Chigwell nor Theydon Bois. But that part of Essex was, in his foster father's words, *"An affluent area where people aren't afraid to splash the cash."* It was an ideal location for a man whose primary business required a legitimate way of cleaning up money.

John had several bars in various parts of London, and he even owned a little country pub on the South Coast that he visited every few months. John enjoyed the lord-like welcome he received when he arrived there with his flavour of the month, which usually came in the form of a blond half his age with a coke habit.

Harvey opened the door without knocking and walked into John's office.

"Alright, Son? Take a seat," said John.

Only three people were allowed to enter the office unannounced.

The first was Sergio, who acted as an adviser to the family. He kept the books and was often the face of the firm in their more legitimate business dealings. Occupying the office next door, Sergio typically used the no-knock rule because he was in and out of John's office all day. It was practical.

The second person was Donny, Harvey's foster brother. Donny worked in John's bars and kept the businesses running on the ground. He entered without knocking, not because his office was close by, but just because he could. It was a display of power in front of John's staff. And it fed Donny's ego.

Harvey didn't knock because he refused to feed people's egos, no matter who they were.

Hearing Harvey arrive, Sergio stepped out of his office into John's, settling into a seat at the side of the room with his laptop. Sergio was a lean man, bordering skinny, of Eastern European descent. His taste for immaculately crafted, tailor-made suits and fine Italian shoes gave off a strong impression. But it was countered by his small frame and spineless whisperings into John's ear. He also had a knack for knowing everything. By placing himself in the middle of any conversation, he guided the firm, whereas John only told it where to go. Sergio was the only one who had the power to coerce John into his way of thinking. John trusted him, as did the other, more silent, partners. He was a safe pair of hands with a massively intelligent head on his shoulders. Sergio was a strategist.

And Harvey loathed him.

Unlike the bar staff, managers, heavies and runners that all worked for John, it was only Harvey who *openly* detested Sergio. Many distrusted him, but Harvey had grown to hate the man. He had been around ever since Harvey was a child, always there in the background, sneaking around, whispering and manipulating.

Sergio always kept a sly and watchful eye on Harvey. Harvey couldn't explain his feeling. It was more of a gut instinct than tangible reasoning. But Sergio shrank when Harvey was around. He averted his eyes as if Harvey could see what he was thinking. That was what bothered Harvey the most; he was always planning.

"Did it go alright? Were there any problems?" Sergio asked Harvey with a little cock of his head.

"No problems. It was easy. In and out," replied Harvey without looking at him.

"Good, and what about the truck?" asked Sergio.

"It was loaded up and driven off. No questions. Two blokes drove off in it. I didn't see their faces," said Harvey.

"Perfect. And did you-"

"Make a statement, Sergio?" finished Harvey. "We did what we could with the resources available to us." Harvey continued to stare at John but could feel Sergio's eyes boring into him.

"There may be some backlash coming from this," warned Sergio. "It'll get noisy before it gets quiet. But not until after the funeral. We should be ready."

"It'll get noisy before it gets quiet? You just started a *war*," said Harvey. He was unable to look in Sergio's direction. Instead, Harvey looked up at the ceiling and took a deep breath, sensing the confusion growing on his foster father's face. "What do you think the Thomsons are going to do now? They're not going to sit on their backsides feeling sorry for themselves. They'll be planning a genocide and they certainly won't wait until after the funeral."

"Sergio, what exactly did you ask Harvey and Julios to do?" asked John, leaning forward. John sat in a large, leather, reclining office chair, and he commanded the room.

"You mean *you* don't know?" asked Harvey.

"Exactly what I told you, John," said Sergio. "We took care of one of Thomson's men. We need them busy. We need them distracted while we-"

"You *don't* know, do you?" said Harvey to John, cutting off Sergio.

"Someone is going to tell me in the next three seconds," John replied, his eyes widening. John kept his cool, a trait for which he was notorious. But he looked between the two men with a rage growing behind his calm exterior.

"My contacts assure me that Terry Thomson will be far too distraught to continue pursuing any other job while he is in mourn-"

"The man is a cold-blooded killer and a businessman, Sergio." The weak justification from Sergio for killing a powerful man like Bradley Thomson was too much for Harvey. "You could set Terry Thomson's mother on fire, and he'd still make time to shove your head up your backside *and* see that your family were all strung up by their balls before he even threw a bucket of water over her. You don't understand these people, Sergio. Why don't you go back to your office and do a spreadsheet or whatever the hell it is you do."

"Let me finish," said Sergio, his voice rising in pitch. "My contacts assure me that the family will be too busy running their legitimate businesses to even consider organising a job as big as the northern job."

"What northern job?" asked Harvey.

John slammed his hand down on his desk. The room fell silent, but his voice remained low and calm. "I want to know who it was we killed last night."

Harvey turned away.

Sergio looked defeated.

"It was Bradley," he said quietly.

"*Bradley Thomson?*" John said calmly.

He lifted the papers from his desk and straightened them before creating a neat pile on the corner of the table. He turned in his chair and looked out of the floor-to-ceiling window at the traffic on the street below. Average people driving average cars to average jobs.

"Sergio, leave the room, please. We'll discuss this later." John remained facing the window while Sergio stood and opened the door. But his voice betrayed the anger that was building inside. "Sergio?"

Sergio turned to face John but kept his head lowered like a scolded child.

"Get Donny to up the security on the bars. I imagine Thomson will be looking for blood. But he might decide to hurt my pocket before the bloodbath starts."

When the door was pulled closed, John turned back to face Harvey.

"I thought you'd know," said Harvey. "Sergio said it was all part of a plan."

"It's not your fault, Son. But you're right. Thomson is going be spitting fire right now, and we need to be crystal on what we're going to do about it."

"We?" asked Harvey. "I'd say that was a job for Sergio. *He* spilt the milk."

The two men locked stares until John broke away. Although his foster father held the power, Harvey was resolute and had no qualms about voicing his opinion, especially against Sergio.

"Listen, Harvey, there's something we need to take care of later this week," said John. His voice had dropped to a gravelly whisper. "It's an important job, but in light of all this, it'll be dangerous. I don't want to talk about it here, but you and Julios are going to have to handle it after Sergio's cock-up."

John Cartwright always spoke about problems using the words '*we*' and '*us*,' but Harvey didn't pay any attention to it. It was just his foster father's way of trying to make Harvey feel included in the family business so that he might one day take on more of a leadership role. This was despite Harvey's attempts to remove himself as much as possible.

"Why don't you come over and have dinner with your old man? We can talk about it at home," said John.

"I have plans this afternoon," replied Harvey.

He felt the beast stir inside him at the thought.

"What plans?" asked John.

Harvey didn't reply.

"Shall we say eight o'clock then?" John asked cheerfully as Harvey stood to leave.

There was no point in nodding or agreeing. It wasn't an optional invitation; it was a decision made by his foster father with an informal agreement. Disobeying the instruction would have consequences. Harvey didn't care much for consequences. But he played along with John's games for an easy life.

Harvey respected the old man and admired his control. Deep down, Harvey loved him in his own kind of way. But their relationship was soured by a deep mistrust rooted in the past. It was clear to Harvey that John knew more than he let on. Whenever Harvey raised the topic of Hannah's death or his real parents, the same old story was recited, verbatim. John made no attempt to embellish it or make it believable. He just expected Harvey to carry on as usual. But Harvey could never be sure if the truth was hidden for his own protection or reasons John would rather forget. After all, John had raised Harvey and Hannah as his own, and Harvey wasn't blind to the affection in John's eyes.

It was the affection in John's eyes that had fuelled the rift between Harvey and Donny, his foster brother. Harvey had been twelve years old when his sister, Hannah, had killed herself, leaving Harvey alone and a target of John's attention. But John was a busy man. He'd had only so many hours in the day to dote on his kids, and Harvey started to get the lion's share of the two boys.

Donny had noticed the favouritism, and as siblings often do, he soon began an onslaught of sly attacks on his younger brother. Spitting in his dinner, pushing him down the stairs and locking him in the dark attic were all common occurrences. The incidents were small and Harvey grew resilient to them. But over time, the attacks built up to mutual hatred. Then Harvey grew wiser and stronger, and with Julios' training, he put Donny in his place several times.

Since those days, it was rare that Harvey and Donny were in the same room. Donny, like Sergio, carried a look of fear in his weak eyes and had a knack for keeping away from Harvey. He preferred instead to enjoy his father's wealth and power with cocaine-fuelled nights in his bars with random women by his side.

Harvey left the first-floor office via the metal steps that led out the back of the building. He walked around the side street where his bike was parked and strode through the alleyway, staying close to the fence. It was another of Julios' rules: never create a pattern, never leave a trail, and never let *anybody* get one step ahead of you.

As he swung his leg over his bike, Harvey glanced up at the rear of the building and found Sergio staring back at him from his office window. Even from a distance, Harvey could see a wry smile on his face. Julios' words of advice played on repeat in Harvey's mind.

Sergio was one step ahead.

CHAPTER EIGHT

John Cartwright sat at his desk thinking about Terry Thomson's possible reactions. There was a light knock at the door. It was Sergio's knock. He only knocked when John was angry.

"Enter," said John. He sat up in his chair and straightened the papers on his desk. "Sergio, what's the news?"

John's mood had quietened enough for the monotonous weekly financial report. It was a sly way for Sergio to justify his worth in light of his recent mistake.

"Hello, John," said Sergio, hiding behind the door. "I have the weekly financial reports for you. Do you have time right now?"

The short time alone had given John time to think. Sergio had known John would be fearful of a war with the Thomsons and would have vetoed the hit on Bradley. But John also understood that the distraction was the best way of getting the Thomsons out of the northern job, leaving them to only deal with Stimson. The diamonds from the northern job were Sergio's key to success, and if it went wrong, it was his neck on the line.

"Is it that time already, Sergio?" replied John

He reached for his desk phone and asked his assistant to bring through two coffees. John eyed the tall, lean man in front of him whose long, bony fingers held the printed copies of the firm's financial reports, both the legitimate and the not-so-legitimate. His gaunt face was clean-shaven with pale skin that stretched across high cheekbones, and his large Romany nose held thick-rimmed glasses that magnified his permanently bloodshot eyes.

"Okay, so let's start with the BVI report," began Sergio.

His faint Eastern European accent added a little romance to the otherwise dull conversation that was about to ensue. The British

Virgin Islands report was a holistic view of the legitimate businesses that were grouped under a BVI holding company, which, being tax-exempt, saved John thousands each year.

"We transferred clean assets-"

"Where's Donny?" John interrupted.

Sergio paused. "I haven't seen him since we landed from our trip."

"I want him to be here for the weekly reports. He needs to know what's going on. Does he even know you're here?" As he spoke, John was reaching for the desk phone. "Get me Donny, please. Call back is fine."

"You would like me to wait, John?" asked Sergio.

The door opened and John's assistant walked in with a tray holding two espressos in small cups sat atop two large saucers, each with an expensive-looking Italian biscuit on the side. They were a touch previously added by Sergio, and a sign of his impeccable taste.

"Thank you, May," said John as the door closed. "No, Sergio. Give me the BVI report then wait for Donny to give the rest."

"Okay. So July saw a ten per cent-"

The desk phone rang. John answered and was connected to Donny by May.

"Where are you, Son?"

"I'm in Wembley, Dad. Just doing an audit of the stock here. Sergio gave me a heads-up that an FSA inspection is likely."

John was used to the Food Standards Agency showing up unannounced.

"Did Sergio also give you a heads-up that today was report day? And is that why you decided to saunter off to the other side of London? Sergio is here now. Why don't you come and join us? You are, after all, the operations manager."

"What about the inspection?"

"You earned five hundred grand last year, Son. Did you earn that by counting bottles and frozen burgers or by making sure the fire extinguishers work? No. You earned it by making sure the business is profitable. I'll see you in less than an hour."

John replaced the handset and gestured for Sergio to continue.

"Okay. We transferred everything we could off-shore, but we still have the clean-"

The phone rang again. John answered.

"There's a gentleman on the line who would like to talk with you."

"Who is it, May?"

"I'm afraid he wouldn't give a name. But he said you'd be keen to hear from him."

"Alright. Put him through."

John motioned for Sergio to hold on and pushed the loudspeaker button. Sergio sank back in his chair, crossed his legs, and unlocked his phone. He tapped on the screen while John spoke, but he listened carefully. He always listened carefully.

"Cartwright," said John cautiously.

"The one and only John Cartwright?" On the other end of the line, the gravelly voice hinted at humour but the tone was far from it.

"That must be the one and only Terry Thomson. To what do I owe the pleasure?"

"Well, you know how it is, John. We're in the same game. I thought I'd give you a call and see how business is going."

"No, Terry. I don't know how it is. We seem to of managed to get this far without standing on each other's toes. Why change all that now?"

"Are you planning something, John? Be straight with me."

"The only thing I'm planning on doing, Terry, is putting the phone down and getting on with my busy day. Take care, Mr Thomson."

"Hang on, hang on," said Terry, the urgency in his voice betraying a momentary lapse of dignity and composure. "Are you there, John?"

"Yeah, I am."

"He's gone, John," said Terry. "Bradley. Did you hear?"

John waited a few seconds as if in shock. He sat back in his chair, lifted his feet to the edge of his desk, and closed his eyes, imagining Terry and the pain of his lifelong enemy. "No, Terry. I didn't hear."

"John, I've got to ask." Terry's voice was clear and strong but wounded. "Was it your lot? Cause if it weren't then it could only be one other firm, and this isn't their style."

"I'm going to be polite given the circumstance, Terry. But don't you ever dare to ask me that question again. I'll ask the boys to keep their ears to the ground. If I hear anything, you'll be the first to know."

John disconnected the call

"He fell for it?" asked Sergio.

"He did. Well, for your sake, Sergio, I hope he did."

CHAPTER NINE

Terry Thomson disconnected the call and sat staring at the phone.

"Lying bastard," he said to the empty room.

He snatched open the top drawer of his desk and lifted the false bottom up to reveal his SIG Sauer P226. It was tucked neatly into a custom-made, felt-lined panel. He slid the handgun from where it had sat untouched for over a year, released the magazine to check it wasn't loaded, and slotted it back into place with a click. Sliding back the action, he looked inside the empty chamber then laid the handgun on his desk and placed his hands in front of him. He closed his eyes and breathed, slow and deep, controlling the whirlwind of scenarios that rushed through his mind. But each time he slowed his thoughts, a picture of Bradley came into view and his anger soared once more.

His meditation was disturbed by a gentle knock at the door. He wasn't in the mood for company, conversation or consolation and ignored the disruption, preferring silence so he could think about possible suspects and reasons for them to do this to him. It was, after all, an attack on him, even if he hadn't been the target. Bradley had been his eldest child and the only son in the business. Terry's other son, Spencer, had chosen to live a normal life removed from the money, adrenaline and risk, a normal life, in which paying off the police and putting hits on other families weren't topics of discussion over breakfast.

Terry would need to call Spencer and tell him the bad news about his brother. He hadn't spoken to him in years. Last time, their father and son chat had ended in a heated exchange of spiteful words, slammed car doors and unanswered calls. Terry had given up after several weeks of persistent attempts. Gradually, they'd drifted apart. He didn't even know where his son was now. But Lenny might. They had been fairly close when the boys were younger. He'd ask Lenny.

As if on cue, there was another gentle knock at the door.

"Who is it?" called Terry.

"It's Lenny, Terry. Just seeing if you're okay. Do you want a cup of tea or something?"

"Come in, Len, will you?"

Terry picked up his handgun once more and began to imagine a faceless man beaten beyond recognition, on his knees and crying for mercy with the muzzle of the Sig between his teeth. Somewhere close by, the door opened and closed, and Lenny sat in the chair opposite Terry.

"What is it, boss?" asked Lenny, snapping Terry from his distant musings on murder.

"Why would somebody kill *Bradley*? Why now?"

"We're trying to find out, Terry," said Lenny. "Honest, mate. I've got all the boys on it."

"What about the guns?"

"We're off-loading half of them to Cartwright in a couple of days. We were going to use the rest for the northern job then ditch them when we're done."

Terry nodded his slow, contemplative nod as he aimed along the barrel of his SIG at a small mark on the wall.

"Killing a man's son is something somebody does to initiate a war, Lenny," said Terry. "Any man worth his salt does not kill a man's flesh and blood as a mere distraction."

"Agreed, Terry."

"And we have to remember that Stimson is not a killer." Terry raised his index finger as if to support the statement.

"Unless that was the point, Terry," said Lenny.

"What do you mean?"

"Well, we're selling Cartwright a dozen MP5s in a couple of days. Why would he hit us so close to a deal?"

"That's what I was wondering," said Terry.

"So if Stimson thinks that all eyes would be on Cartwright because he's the obvious suspect, that would leave Stimson free to go and do the northern job."

"I see. Smart thinking, Lenny," said Terry. He sat back in his chair and let the weight of his head fall onto the headrest. "So you think Stimson *was* trying to start a war between us and the Cartwrights?"

"He must be," said Lenny.

"Smart bastard," replied Terry.

The theory did make perfect sense. Cartwright was supposed to be buying twelve Heckler and Koch MP5s from Terry later that week. There was no way John Cartwright would kill Bradley before they did a deal.

"John Cartwright and I weren't always enemies, you know?" said Terry. "We've always run our own firms and didn't always see eye to eye, but in the beginning, we weren't at war. He kept to his turf. I kept to mine. There was an understanding."

"So what happened?" asked Lenny.

Terry exhaled, long and slow.

"The usual," he replied. "Greed, I guess. He got in my way. I got in his way. It was the eighties. Gang wars were kicking off all over the place. But before that, we'd trade all the time. He sold me a box of shotguns once in return for some inside information on a job he was planning."

"What's he like then?"

"He's as hard as they come and smarter

than most," replied Terry. "The only thing he lacks is vision. That's why he still run bars and pubs. The real money is in the clubs. Everyone knows that."

"So why now?" asked Lenny. "Why is he buying guns from us now?"

"I wanted to see if he was planning the northern job, Lenny. A mutual friend of ours set it up for me. See, I knew that if I offered John Cartwright twelve of our lovely MP5s at a higher than average price, he'd be planning the northern job."

"But how does that help us, Terry?" asked Lenny. "I mean, if we sell Cartwright the guns, he'll be just as well equipped to do the job as us."

"Do you know how many years you'd get for possession of twelve automatic weapons, Lenny?"

"You're setting them up?" said Lenny with a smile and laughed out loud at the plan.

"Having them buy the guns from me was the only way I could be sure of them being in a certain place at a certain time with a box of guns. It's not rocket science, Lenny," said Terry, staring at the ceiling, pleased with his plan.

"What do you want to do now then?" asked Lenny, once more dragging Terry out of his own thoughts.

"Well, we can go back and forth like this all night, Lenny, but neither one of us can do anything but speculate, can we?"

"Not really, no, Terry. It could've been Stimson or Cartwright. They both have the method, means and motive."

"Right then," said Terry, pushing himself out of his chair. He stepped to one side to view himself in the full-length mirror fixed to the wall beside the window then straightened his suit, admiring the contrast between his tan and the whiter-than-white shirt. "So there's only one thing we can do, isn't there, Lenny?"

"What's that, boss?"

Terry turned to face the much younger man, adjusted his cuffs and collected the gun from the desk.

"We'll kill the bleeding pair of them. One of them wanted a war, and a war is what they'll get. If we don't retaliate, we'll be seen as weak."

He turned back to the mirror and continued to admire his reflection, now with the addition of the SIG.

"And Terry Thomson is not weak."

"What about the guns?" asked Lenny, recognising the fire in his boss' eyes.

"Here's what's going to happen. Step one, find me Donny Cartwright. Take him down and make it public. Make a mess but make sure he's recognisable. As long as John Cartwright denies the hit on Bradley, I'll deny the hit on Donny. It'll be a stalemate."

"Right."

But Lenny was a little unsure of the move.

"Step two, the gun deal is still on. John Cartwright won't back down. I know him. He'll send his best men and they'll want to take us out at the deal. If they do, we'll be ready. I've got just the man up my sleeve."

"What about Stimson?" asked Lenny.

"We won't see Stimson until the diamonds are in Britain. No doubt, he'll dig a tunnel or do something extravagant to steal them. And when he comes out, we'll be standing right there with twelve lovely MP5s ready to take those nice shiny diamonds off him, won't we? That's step three."

"That's a big risk, Terry," said Lenny. "Cartwright's men are pretty heavy."

"What are you saying? Don't you want the job, Lenny?"

"I'm not saying that at all. But if me and Rob get hit, the firm gets an awful lot smaller."

"I trust you, Lenny, and I trust Rob. That's why I'm sending you."

"What about if we had a driver? I'd manage him. All he'd have to do is drive the van, give them the guns and take the cash. If he doesn't get shot, he's a lucky boy. If he does, well, we'll still have twelve MP5s to do the northern job. Plus, John Cartwright would have just started the war by openly killing our man."

"Kind of like a fall guy, you mean?" said Terry. "Expendable?"

"Yeah. Rob and I will be close by to see it all go down, but far enough away to survive."

"I like it," said Terry. "Who do you have in mind?"

"I'll find someone expendable. Who do *you* have in mind to take care of the Cartwrights?"

"As I said, Lenny, I know just the man for the job." Once again, Terry sighted the mark on the wall along the stubby barrel of his SIG.

"How about that cup of tea? I'm suddenly feeling quite rejuvenated."

Supportive to the core, Lenny nodded at the master plan and headed for the door to the kitchen. Terry checked he was out of earshot then picked up his phone and dialled a number from memory. It was a number he hadn't dialled for a very long time.

"Frank, my old friend, how have you been?"

CHAPTER TEN

"There's been a total of four deaths by garrotting in London during the past year, sir," said Mills. "Only one of the cases is closed and the suspect is currently serving fifteen years in Belmarsh."

"And the other three?" asked Frank.

"Unsolved, sir. Gang crime. Lots of tight lips and fat wallets."

"What about the motorbike? Did we find anything?"

"We did, sir," said Melody. But her tone had shifted; her competence had faded to insecurity.

"Go on, Mills."

"We matched the tyre tread to three unsolved murders."

"So that's good news," said Frank. "We have a lead?"

"Not so good, sir. We've been hunting the killer for more than a decade."

"What do we know about him?" asked Frank, intrigued by the potential new challenge.

"All we know is that he targets sex offenders."

"A vigilante?" said Frank.

"This is no ordinary vigilante, sir," continued Mills. "The man is sick."

"Dying sick?"

Mills shook her head.

"Twisted sick, sir. The cases were never made public. The top brass was worried the locals would support the killer if they found out. They'd give him a name and then, of course, the copycats would come out of the woodwork."

"So you're telling me there's some psycho out there murdering sex offenders and nobody is doing anything about it? How do we know it's the same guy?"

Mills hesitated then passed Frank a blue

file. Inside were photographs printed on eight-by-six photo paper. The first showed the remains of a man lying on a forest floor with only stumps where his limbs had been. His remaining skin was charred beyond recognition. The second photo showed the peeled face of a skinless man.

Frank snapped the folder shut and passed it back to Mills.

"He's sick alright."

"Psychologist's report classes him as a primary psychopath. He'll exhibit no emotion and won't respond to punishment, possibly as the result of child abuse or traumatisation. He most likely grew up in a violent household. He's deeply scarred, sir."

"Aren't we all, Mills?" said Frank. But the look on Mills' face discouraged Frank's flippant response. "And we think this man killed Bradley Thomson, do we?"

"Can I be honest, sir?"

"Of course."

"I hope not. I really do."

The fear in Mills' eyes added a heavy sincerity to her words. But their shared moment was cut short by the flashing screen of Frank's phone, which began to vibrate on his desk.

"Would you excuse me?" said Frank. As she was closing the door, he called out to her. "Mills?"

"Sir?" she said, half in and half out of his office.

"Good work."

"Thank you, sir," she replied and closed the door.

Frank hit the green button to answer the call.

"Carver."

"Frank, my old friend, how have you been?"

"I wondered when you'd call," replied Frank, feeling a wave of nausea wash over him.

"Yeah, well, it's been a bit busy. You know how it is, Frank," replied Terry. His thick East London accent suited his gruff tone, but somehow, he still managed to sound clear and articulate. "I've got a job for you."

"A job?" said Frank. "And what makes you think I'm for hire?"

"Well, Frank, there's still the matter of your little debt, and I know exactly how you can repay me."

"I repaid that debt a long time ago."

"You repaid nothing, Frank," said Terry. "I'll tell you when the debt is paid."

Frank was silent.

"Yeah. You remember, don't you?"

"It's been over a year, Terry."

"And now your time has come. I always knew you'd come in handy one day, Frank."

"What's the job?"

"Babysitter," said Terry.

"I'm a little long in the tooth for babysitting."

"Well, it's a little more than that if I'm being honest."

"Spit it out, Terry. I'm a busy man."

"I'm doing a deal. I want you to make sure it goes smooth and my boys don't get hurt."

"Where's the deal?" asked Frank.

"In the sticks somewhere. I'll have someone send you the location. It'll be discreet."

"What's the deal?"

"It's a box, Frank. Do you need to know any more than that?" said Terry.

"Who's the buyer?"

"That's a bit direct, Frank."

"Should I fluff it up a little for you?" asked

Frank. "You want me to stroke your ego, Terry?"

"Why do you want to know who the buyer is?"

"Self-preservation, Terry."

"Self-preservation, Frank?"

"Self-preservation. If you tell me the buyers are three little old ladies, I'll know where I stand. But if you tell me you're doing a deal with the Essex arm of ISIS, then I might need to adjust my approach."

"It's neither."

"I was hoping for old ladies."

"You like old ladies, Frank?"

"They make good tea, Terry."

"It's not old ladies, Frank."

"So no tea then?"

"No tea."

"Are you going to tell me?" asked Frank. "You've built it up now."

"Did I build it up or did you?" replied Terry. "I recall it was you that asked the question, Frank."

"And it's you who's been avoiding the answer."

"Cartwright."

"John Cartwright?" Frank sat forward in

his chair and lowered his voice. "Are you crazy?"

"The one and only. Feel better?"

"Well, I know where I stand. That's all I wanted." Frank paused. "Terry?"

"Yes, Frank."

"This is the last time. I've repaid the debt."

"Are you severing our relationship, Frank?"

"No, not severing. But I won't be in your pocket after this one."

"One of my men took the rap for you if you remember, Carver. You don't get to make demands."

"It's been long enough," said Frank. "I'm retiring soon. I'd like to actually live that long."

Terry was quiet for a moment.

"Alright, Frank. I understand."

"You do?" said Frank.

"Yeah, of course. I'd like to put my feet up one day myself."

His feet had never been down in the first place, thought Frank.

"Course, there's a price to pay for that kind of freedom," said Terry.

"A price?"

"For freedom."

"Is that right?"

Here it comes, thought Frank.

"That's the rules," said Terry. "How badly do you want to retire?"

"Don't play games, Terry. Spit it out."

"I suppose you know already, don't you?"

"Depends on what it is you suppose I already know, Terry."

"Bradley. My boy."

"What about him?"

"He was hit, Frank. Did you know?"

Terry paused to listen to Frank's reaction.

"No," Frank lied.

"Adam Stimson got him."

"You sure about that, Terry?" asked Frank. "That doesn't sound like Stimson's style."

"You came to that conclusion quickly, Frank. Sounds like you already gave it some thought."

"It's my job to see through the crap, Terry. I'm sorry to hear about it, anyway."

"Yeah, well. It doesn't end here."

"And this is where I come in, is it?" asked Frank.

"When the deal is done, I want you to off the Cartwrights."

"You want me to what?" Frank stopped himself from shouting it aloud and whispered into the phone, "You want me to kill John Cartwright? Are you insane?"

"Careful, Frank. We're friends but let's not throw insults around."

"We're not friends, Terry. We're two people on two very different paths if that's what you think I'm going to do."

"I don't need you to off John himself. But I do need his men sorted out. Just whoever turns up at the gun deal. My man gives them the guns. Their man gives my man the money. My guy drives off. You take the Cartwrights down. Plus, as a sweetener, you get to keep the guns. I imagine there's a whole team of you somewhere searching for them."

"So it's guns, is it?" said Frank.

"A box of them, Frank."

"And why do you have a big box of guns? You're planning a job, aren't you?"

"Our relationship doesn't go quite that far, Frank. Let's stay on track, shall we?"

"You make it sound so easy," said Frank.

"But I thought you said it was Adam Stimson's boys that got to Bradley?"

"Well it's not rocket science, is it?" said Terry. "Stimson's trying to start a war, and Cartwright's buying my guns because he wants to play with the big boys."

"So you take out the Cartwrights and Stimson thinks you fell for it."

"You're learning."

"Meanwhile, Cartwright doesn't interfere in the job you're planning, and Stimson walks right into your hands."

"Everyone's a winner, Frank," said Terry. "Well, everyone that counts."

"Right."

"You know what to do, Frank?"

"I do now. Then we're done. That's it. This is over."

"Oh, Frank, I nearly forgot."

Terry wanted to add a final power play.

"What is it, Terry?"

"Don't try anything stupid."

"Of course not," said Frank.

But Terry had already hung up.

CHAPTER ELEVEN

In an interview room at Potters Bar police station in North London, Shaun Tyson held his hands out. A begrudging officer removed his handcuffs with a stony expression and rough manner that did little to mask his opinion of Shaun. As Shaun rubbed at the red marks on his wrists, he was led to a small stack of blue, yellow and white papers on the desk of the duty officer. A pen attached to a curled flexible cord was dropped beside them.

Three stars had been made beside the areas where Shaun was to sign. But he received no verbal instruction. Hate-filled eyes stabbed at his conscience from all corners of the room. The officer behind the duty counter, two more behind a meshed security window, and another tall, dark officer were all watching him with silent loathing.

The conditional release form was justified in blue handwriting. It agreed that Shaun's court date was pending and insufficient evidence prohibited him from being detained any longer. But Shaun knew it wouldn't be long before the court heard what they needed to hear. The idea of a grim-faced judge slamming his hammer played over in his mind as Shaun signed his name with an unsteady hand.

"We'll be in touch, Mr Tyson."

The officer punched in a security code and shoved open the heavy door when its magnetic release sounded. The loud, buzzing alarm caught the attention of the few people waiting in a row of blue, plastic reception chairs.

"Mr Tyson?"

Shaun turned and stared up at the officer holding the door.

"I'd advise you to get yourself home as quick as you can."

He'd been locked up long enough for word to spread. His face had no doubt been on the local news. All it would take was for one angry local to recognise him and start an onslaught of retribution.

"Yes," he replied. "Thank you."

The cold afternoon and a heightened sense of fear sent a shiver through Shaun's core. His rapid heartbeat brought a thin layer of sweat to his pores, which caught the sharp wind and stiffened his shaking limbs. He pulled the hood of his sweatshirt up and around his face, both for warmth and to avoid recognition.

A small group of teenagers ambled past. They smoked cigarettes and laughed the loud, uncaring laughs of youths with nothing to fear. One of them glanced back at Shaun, catching his eye. But the look was fleeting and Shaun hoped he hadn't been recognised.

A steady stream of traffic passed left and right on the main road. But Shaun noticed a static shape among the movement. One hundred yards away on the far side of the street, parked beside an old, black taxi, a man was sitting on a motorcycle dressed in a black leather jacket and staring directly at Shaun. A curl of faint, grey smoke was hanging in the air beside the bike's exhaust. With one gloved hand, the rider lowered down his black visor.

The three teenagers who had passed him stopped further down the road. They huddled together as if in conference and stared back at Shaun, whose heart was working overtime. Inside the pockets of his hooded sweatshirt, his long fingers rubbed his sweaty palms with anxiety.

Shaun glanced back across the road at the rider, but he was gone. He searched the traffic left and right, but there was no sign of the bike. There were no exhaust fumes. No man in black was anywhere to be seen.

The teenagers began to walk towards Shaun, slowly at first. But it was enough for Shaun to start moving. He turned left, kept his head down, and worked out what route he would take to get home. A network of back alleys could be reached from the next side street. As he turned, he glanced back at the teenagers. They had quickened their pace. One of them was using his phone, maybe calling his friends.

With the empty side street ahead of him, Shaun started to run.

The fear that coursed through his body had taken control of his legs, slowing him. No matter how hard he pushed, his legs felt alien. He glanced back. The teenagers were running too, and they were fast. Shaun searched the road ahead, seeking an exit. Two more youths had turned into the street and were pointing at Shaun from just three hundred yards away. He looked back once more, but stumbled, fell and rolled onto the ground. It was just like a dream he'd had the previous night in the police cell.

He closed his eyes, preparing himself for the inevitable beating. But as the footsteps thundered closer and his heart beat like a drum, the growl of an engine came to a stop beside where he lay curled up in a ball.

"Get in," said a voice.

Shaun opened his eyes and found a white unmarked van parked in the road beside where he was standing. The side door was open.

"No," said Shaun. "No, please."

He scurried away from the road. The teenagers were closing in from both sides. The van was in front. It was over. A loud sob rose from his stomach and fell from his lips. It was like no other sound he'd ever made before.

"Get in the van, Shaun," said the man again. Shaun looked back at the running teenagers. "Seriously, mate, I won't ask you again. Get in the van. You've got about ten seconds." The man's voice was growing agitated.

"Who are you? How do you know my name? You can't expect me to just climb into the back of a van," said Shaun. His voice was high and loud. Maybe a neighbour would hear it and help him.

"Shaun, we are here to *stop* you getting into any more trouble. Do you *know* what those boys are going to do to you?"

Shaun nodded.

"Do you want help?"

Another nod and a flash of hope, warm and bright.

"So get in the van."

The man wound up his window as a sign that the discussion was over. The two groups of boys were closing in on either side, sprinting towards Shaun. It was now or never.

Three steps on shaky legs and Shaun fell into the back of the van. He dropped to the wooden floor in a corner and curled up, ready for the blows. But instead, the side door was slammed shut and the loud diesel engine roared into life, low and angry above the shouts of the teenagers, who had missed their target by just a few seconds. A few hurled stones at the sides of the van, but the driver didn't slow.

The pitch darkness in the rear cargo area offered a space of relief and calm. Shaun found a wheel arch to sit on and allowed his racing heart to wind down. Out of the frying pan and into the fire, he thought to himself.

The journey seemed endless, but at least the driving was calm. There were no sudden turns and only gentle braking. Imagining the network of roads, Shaun tried to guess where they were taking him, but small turns here and there blurred his imagination. Then they hit the M25 motorway and the back of the van filled with the grumble of the diesel engine and the incessant rumble of the road.

Shaun had spent more than an hour sitting alone in the darkness with his thoughts, regrets and wild imagination when the van slowed and pulled off the motorway. Then the turns were tighter and sharper and the hills were more defined. A part of Shaun, the coward that tugged at his heart and fed his mind with possibilities, hoped the journey would last longer, maybe forever. He was safe in the van. Nobody could touch him, and he could touch nobody.

But after a few more minutes of winding roads, Shaun felt the van slow once more. It then turned onto a bumpy surface where it finally shuddered to a stop.

The silence was agonising.

Once again, Shaun's tired heart started to beat wildly. The layer of sweat resumed its position on the palms of his hands and under his arms. He could smell himself. It was as if his carnal senses were heightened like that of a deer circled by wolves. He smelt the oily odour of diesel, the grain of the van's wooden floor, and most of all, the steely scent of his own fear.

Bright light filled the van as the door screeched open, breaking the security of silence.

"Out," said the dark silhouette of the man.

Shaun hesitated, afraid to move.

"Are you deaf or something? *Out!*"

Shaun heard the driver call out from the

other side of the van, "Come on, Lenny. What are you playing at?"

"It's not *me*. I can't get *him* out of the van. It took him bleeding long enough to get in and now he won't get out."

"Well tell him he can sleep in there if he wants. Or he can come inside and have a nice cup of tea."

The man at the door spoke quietly. Shaun's eyes were beginning to adjust to the light so he could see the man's face more clearly.

"Mate, we're not going to hurt you. We're going to help you. Trust me."

The man offered out his hand to help Shaun.

"Come on."

And then it came. Like a pressure valve releasing a cloud of angry steam into the atmosphere, all his hopes, prayers, and desperate clutches to possibilities succumbed to the bitter reality that there was no escape. Then it faded, leaving Shaun with a single choice.

He pushed himself to his feet with trepidation and dropped down onto the gravel.

Unsteady on his shaking legs, he held onto the door and took in his surroundings.

"Where are we?" he asked, his voice more of a breath than a vocalised sound.

"You'll see. This way."

The man slammed the van door and headed towards a single-floor building. It was the rightmost of three structures that had been built in a crude C-shape to form a court-yard. The centre building appeared to be an old farmhouse with two floors and eight large windows. The left-side building was a double garage.

"Come on, Shaun," called the man from the door of the building.

"I'm coming," said Shaun.

He allowed himself one more look at the endless sky above.

"I'm ready," he whispered to himself.

CHAPTER TWELVE

From the top of the hill, surrounded by fields and trees, Harvey watched the white van take a left turn off the quiet country lane. The driver slowed and pulled into the grounds of the only building in sight, which was an old farmhouse. Harvey killed the bike's engine and removed his helmet as Shaun Tyson was led from the van into the building on the right. It looked like a small barn that had been converted into living space or offices. Across the open fields, the sound of the slamming sliding door disturbed a few birds that took to the air. They circled once and then returned to the ground to nest or feed when the silence of nature resumed.

The autumn day was drawing to a close. The temperature was already dropping and long shadows of the bare trees reached across the fields like long fingers searching for warmth. A small gap in the hedgerow to Harvey's right opened onto a patch of mud beneath an elm tree. It was the perfect place to store his bike and wait for darkness while watching for movement in the farmhouse.

As time went by, lights from the building flicked on, lighting the courtyard. Two men carried a large wooden crate from the van to the open garage. But Shaun Tyson was nowhere to be seen.

When darkness had fallen, Harvey made his way along the lane at the top of the hill to gain a better view of the small development. He passed the turning that led down the hill and continued on straight to see the rear of the house where a ten-foot brick wall and tall conifer trees blocked any view. But Harvey saw a single light shining in the rear garden.

The house backed onto fields, which may or may not have belonged to the property. It was common for small plots of farming land to be sold off. With no farming machinery in view or space to keep it, Harvey assumed the small plot of land was isolated. Keeping to the edges of the field and the clumps of grass alongside a drainage ditch, Harvey made his way to the rear of the house. Two large gates were locked with a chain.

He pushed on one of the gates and it opened to the extent of the chain. It allowed a twelve-inch gap, enough for him to slip through. Then Harvey began Julios' standard one-minute wait in case the noise had alerted somebody. The rear garden, shielded by tall conifers, enjoyed near darkness. Only the light from a single window shone across the tips of a row of wildflowers.

A full minute passed before Harvey made his way behind the trees, creeping along the wall towards the single light. It called to him. The window belonged to a small bedroom as wide as two beds and twice as long, which Harvey guessed to be a guest room for the farmhouse. It was furnished with minimal effort, hosting a single bed and a wall-mounted TV above a small desk.

A shadow danced across the room then disappeared.

Harvey waited.

Then, as if sensing Harvey's presence, the

shadow gave way to a human form, who moved to the window and searched the night with wondering eyes.

Harvey froze.

The man drew the thin net curtains to one side, glanced back at the door, then tried to open the window. But it was locked. He stared out into the darkness at the sky above and towards the trees as if it were all new. Then, without warning, he stared straight at where Harvey was standing in the shadows. The man's face was loathsome and red from tears. His eyes strained from lack of sleep and his tongue rested between his parted lips giving him a perverse yet naïve appearance.

"Found you," Harvey whispered.

CHAPTER THIRTEEN

"Not thinking of trying to run for it, are you?"

Shaun turned from the window and found Lenny standing in the doorway.

"No," replied Shaun. "I wasn't. I wouldn't."

"Nothing is stopping you," said Lenny. He took a step closer. A cruel smile spread across his gaunt face, and he gestured to the darkness outside. "But you're safer in here with us than out there."

"I won't run," said Shaun. "I don't even know where I am."

"You don't need to know," said Lenny, turning to leave the room. "Anyway, the boss wants to see you."

Taking slow, tentative steps, Shaun left the relative safety of his new accommodation and followed Lenny along the small hallway. At the end of it was the entrance to the central building. But Lenny disappeared through a door on the right then poked his head back into the hallway a few seconds later.

"Come on. Hurry up."

Shaun took a few deep breaths and walked through the door into a long room with soft, red, leather couches, a coffee table, and a large desk at one end. Behind the desk, sitting with his hands clasped together, a thin, older man wearing a white, open-collared shirt was sitting and staring at Shaun.

"Take a seat, Shaun," said the wiry old man whose thick horn-rimmed glasses magnified his dark eyes and suggested a calculating yet brutal intelligence. He offered Shaun the seat with an open palm. It was an indication that he should sit in that particular seat and no other.

"Lenny tells me you often need telling more than once, and that maybe you're a bit slow. Well, Shaun, my old son, I'll tell you this once, so listen very carefully." The old man cleared his throat, but his gravelly tones remained. "*I* do not intend on repeating *anything* I say just so that you can stand and stare at me. *Understood?*"

Shaun nodded.

"Good. Now sit down, shut up and listen."

Shaun sat in the offered seat and placed his hands on his lap as if he were being interviewed.

"Good. We're making progress," said the man. "Do you want a cup of tea?"

"No, thank you, sir," Shaun replied quietly.

"Lenny, get him a cup of tea, will you?" said the man, ignoring Shaun's response.

Lenny rose and left the room by another side door, leaving just the man and Shaun at the desk. The driver of the van sat on one of the red leather sofas in the corner of the room, playing with his phone. The old man sat forward, put his elbows on the surface of the desk, and linked his fingers, resting them against his mouth.

"Tell me about yourself, Shaun," he said.

"About myself?"

"Don't make me repeat myself, Shaun,"

the old man warned, and he raised a bony index finger.

"I'm twenty-four."

"That's a start. How about embellishing on that very detailed account?"

"I'm from North London, but I live in Potters Bar now. My dad left, and Mum moved us up there for a fresh start."

"You live with your mum, do you?"

"Yeah," said Shaun.

He was slightly embarrassed that he hadn't managed to leave the family nest at his age.

"And why did your dad leave, Shaun?"

"Dunno. I don't think he had another woman. But him and mum always argued. He just never came home one time."

"That's a shame, Shaun. Do you see him at all?"

"No. I haven't seen him since he left."

"And how do you feel about that? Would you like to see him?"

"I don't mind, really. I mean, I don't know if *he* wants to see *me*. Especially not now."

"Especially not now? But he's your dad, Shaun. Why wouldn't a father want to see his son?"

"Because of what I did, and because of who I am."

"Tell me about what you did, Shaun. Tell me why the police were holding you."

"You know what I did."

"Do I? All I know is what I read in the papers, and you can't believe everything you read in the papers, can you, Shaun?" The man sat back and folded his arms. "Tell me what you did."

There was an uncomfortable silence before Shaun leaned forward and rested his elbows on his legs. He stared at the wooden floor. His eyes didn't focus or blink. They just followed the intricate patterns of the hardwood's grain.

"Shaun, I'm waiting. Tell me *where* you did it. Let's start there."

"In the forest near our house by the lake."

The man nodded, encouraging Shaun to tell his story. Shaun's urge to tell it grew. It was as if vocalising the events would ease the pressure building inside him.

"I was out walking one time. I liked to walk there. It's quiet. Every now and then, I'd get a couple of beers from the off-licence, and I'd sit there by the lake. If you sit long enough, the birds and squirrels get used to you, and you can watch them running around. One time, I'd finished my beers and was sitting near the lake looking at the swans. There was a voice behind me. A girl's voice. She asked me what I was doing."

CHAPTER FOURTEEN

"Stop snivelling, Shaun. You're going to mess the floor up," said the old man.

Lenny returned with two cups of tea. He handed the first cup to the old man. The second, a mug with the slogan '*World's Best Husband*' on it in bold red letters, he placed on a coaster in front of Shaun.

"Len, get him some tissues, will you? He's making a right old mess over there."

Lenny left once more to fetch a box of tissues from the kitchen. He returned a few seconds later, holding them out for Shaun, who took the box without looking up.

"Do you know what they do to people like you in prison, Shaun?"

Shaun shook his head and continued to stare at the floor.

"Well, put it this way, you wouldn't be doing much of what you did again, mate. Your old boy would be hacked off and fed to E-wing for their supper."

The old man laughed at his own joke. But even amidst the laughter, Shaun could feel his dark eyes burning into him.

"I don't know what would be worse though, to be honest," the old man continued. "They must be hunting you down in Potters Bar right now. I imagine crowds of them are sitting outside your mum's house with pitch-forks. You're lucky we found you so easily. What do you reckon, Rob?" he called to the driver of the van. "Being locked up or being let out? Which one would you prefer?"

"I reckon I'd prefer to off myself, boss, in that scenario," said Rob from the other side of the room. "Let's face it, neither option is likely to make you many friends."

"Too right, Rob. Did you hear that, Shaun? Rob over there reckons you ought to *off* yourself. What do you say to that then?"

"I thought about it," mumbled Shaun through his phlegm-filled throat.

The talk of suicide only made his sobbing worse. His body convulsed as he tried to stop the inevitable. He closed his eyes tight, which screwed up his face, and a thick trail of snot ran down his nose far too fast for any tissue to stop.

"You thought about it, did you? Did you hear that, Rob? He thought about *offing* himself."

"Yeah, we heard, boss. We're amazed he didn't follow through with it. Aren't we, Lenny?"

"That's right. *Amazed*, we are," said Lenny.

"How would you do it, Shaun?" asked Terry. "Here, Rob, how would *you* do it if you was him?"

"Well, it would have to be quick, boss. I reckon jumping off a bridge is a pretty good way to go. They reckon you have a heart attack on the way down. So you don't even feel the bump."

"Jumping off a bridge." Terry said the words staccato. "Shaun, what do you say to that then?"

Shaun didn't reply.

"Lenny, what about you? How would *you*

do it?"

Lenny sat opposite Rob on the couch, looking at his phone.

"Well, I always thought jumping in front of a train would be quick. But it's such a selfish way to go, you know? All those people late home from work. So I reckon it'd have to be drowning. That's it, yeah. They reckon it's quick and one of the better ways to go. Over in seconds. I saw it on a documentary."

"Do they now? One of the better ways to go? Drowning. Did you hear all that, Shaun?" He paused. "Shaun, don't make me repeat myself. I don't like repeating myself."

"I heard it. I heard it all."

The wiry man in the chair leaned forward and said quietly, "So, tell me, Shaun. Tell me how *you* would do it."

Shaun couldn't hold his emotion any longer. A loud whimper escaped from his throat along with a deep breath that culminated in a howl. He cried wildly, unable to restrain the tears that had built up behind his burning eyes.

"I was going to hang myself," Shaun said, mid-sob. "I was going to jump from the balcony in the library and snap my neck. I'd be *done* with it all."

"There we go," said the old man, sitting back in his winged chair. "You were going to *hang* yourself."

The old man sat forward again, intrigued by Shaun's choice of suicide.

"Have you ever seen a man die, Shaun?"

Shaun shook his head.

"No."

The man was silent for a moment.

"I have." He grinned. "I've seen many men die, and you know what, Shaun?" The man raised a single eyebrow. "Pretty much every single one of them pissed their pants. What a way to be remembered, eh? Pissing your pants? Not only would you be remembered for being the nonce that ruined that poor little girl's life, took away her innocence and caused devastation among her family, but they'll all remember that you pissed your pants as well. Not to mention, of course, the nightmares you'd have given the old Doris who unlocks the library every morning. She'd have walked in one day, probably slipped over in your piss, broken her hip, and laid in the stinking puddle looking up at your ugly mug swinging above her. What do you reckon, Rob?"

"I reckon you're right, boss. Slipped over, broke her hip and lay in his piss."

"What do you want from me?" Shaun asked.

"Lenny, tell Shaun the *first* thing I want."

"Courtesy, Shaun," said Lenny.

"That's right, Shaun," said the old man. "Courtesy. A little bit of respect for the man that got you off the street before you were lynched, castrated and set on fire by the locals with their pitchforks. Understood?"

Shaun nodded silently.

"So do me the courtesy of looking me in the eye when you talk to me. I'm fed up of looking at your ear. What's on the floor, anyway?"

"Nothing. There's nothing on the floor," Shaun said, lifting his head to meet the man's eyes.

"Right. Well, stop looking down there and look at me. Can you drive?"

"Eh?"

"A car, Shaun. Can you drive a car? Do you have a driving licence?"

"Yes, I've got one."

Shaun searched for his wallet.

"I don't need to see it, just as long as you've got one. Right. I've got a job coming up and you, my perverted little friend, are going to be very useful to me."

CHAPTER FIFTEEN

"What is it you want me to do?" asked Shaun.

"Oh, it's just a little job. Drop something off for me. Collect something else. You'll know nearer the time. In the meantime, why don't you relax? Watch some TV. Go for a walk if you want. It's nice out there. Proper British countryside."

"What happens after I do this job for you?"

"Shaun, there are three possible outcomes. Being the nice man I am, I'm going to let you decide which one happens."

Terry was growing impatient, but he composed himself well. He explained things to Shaun in a childlike manner so the possibilities were communicated plain and simple.

"One."

Terry leaned forward on the desk and held up the skinny index finger of his right hand. It was often used to accompany his mouth when ordering people around.

"You try to run away, call the police, or mess things up for me in any way, shape or form, then Lenny and Rob will take you outside for a good kicking. After that, they'll dump your broken, pitiful, perverted body on your mum's doorstep. Then either she or the locals can find you. Pitchforks, Shaun. Pitchforks."

He added a middle finger to the first without removing his eyes from Shaun's.

"Two. You ask too many questions. If that habit doesn't stop, the boys will see that my pigs are fed and that you are never seen again. Have you ever seen a pig eat a human body, Shaun?"

Shaun's jaw widened in horror. "No."

"It's quite fascinating. There's no grace to it. They don't care which part they eat first. They're not like you eating your mum's lovely roast dinner on a Sunday in front of the telly.

You eat your greens first to get them out the way so you can savour the tender meat and succulent gravy. But no, Shaun. It's not like that at all. One or two of them will start on your feet or your hands, whichever is closest. Then they'll work their way up your body until nothing is left. They have to grind your bone down with their huge incisors and tear your flesh off. But they seem to manage it okay, and it doesn't take long."

Terry sat back in his chair and studied Shaun's reactions.

"Whereabouts along that process a man actually stops feeling pain and succumbs to death is different every time. Some blokes have survived for ages. Some even watch their knackers getting chomped off, unable to defend themselves because their hands are already eaten. Do you remember that one, Lenny?"

"Yes, boss. I remember. One of my favourites, that was," replied Lenny.

"It's a fascinating thing to watch."

Terry rearranged his finger configuration; he held up three digits, the pinkie, ring and middle, with his palm facing Shaun.

"Three. You relax. Thank God, or whoever you want, that you're not being sodomised in Pentonville Prison right now. Be grateful to walk in the countryside with the fresh air and the chance at starting a new life. In a week, you'll take the van, do a delivery, pick up a bag for me, and come back."

"Then what?"

"*That's* another question, Shaun," said Terry. "Can you remember the outcome of asking too many questions?"

Shaun nodded. "Yes."

"Oink oink, Shauny." Terry turned to his boys. "Lenny, Rob, show him back to his room. Then sort out that box in the garage out, will you?"

"Yes, boss," replied Rob.

"Oh, and Shauny, my old son," said Terry.

Shaun looked back at the man at the desk, whose cruel smile had faded into a warning stare.

"No more questions."

CHAPTER SIXTEEN

John Cartwright stood in the middle of the large kitchen of his five-bedroom house in Theydon Bois. He was chopping onions and carrots with a practised hand at the central unit. His workstation was neat and organised, a reflection of his controlled life and mind.

Harvey leaned on the far side of the island and sipped a glass of water.

"Fancy making yourself useful and getting your old man a brandy?" asked John.

Thankful for the break in monotonous silence and the excuse to leave the room, Harvey stepped into the lounge and walked to the drinks cabinet. He poured half an inch of brandy over three ice cubes in a crystal tumbler. Exactly how the old man liked it.

He sat the brandy by John's hand and resumed his position leaning on the counter.

"Thanks, Son."

"Is anyone else joining us?" asked Harvey.

"No. I thought we could have a night together, you know? Have a little chat."

Harvey didn't reply.

"So how's the bike?" asked John.

"It's fine."

"Why don't you get yourself a car? It must be bloody freezing on that thing."

"It's fine," said Harvey.

"What about the place, you know, in France?"

It was a typical conversation with John. The topic changed from one minute to the next, never delving into details unless, of course, John wanted to hear the details. Then there was no escaping it.

"I'm getting there. No rush."

"Well, there's a job coming up. You could earn big if you want it."

"I told you. I don't want to get involved in all that. I like the little jobs Julios and I do. It's enough for me."

"Yeah, but they're not frequent. You need a regular income. You *need* money so you can make *plans* and buy that little French farm you always wanted."

"The farmhouse will happen. Can we leave it there?"

"Alright, alright. I'm just trying to make sure you've got enough. I'm making sure you're sorted. That's all."

"I know. Where's Donny skiving off these days?" asked Harvey. He was keen to move the conversation away from his life plans. "I haven't seen him creeping around for a while."

"Your brother? He's off somewhere. He said he'd be back tomorrow. He better be. I need him on this job."

"What's the job?" asked Harvey.

"Thought you didn't want in?"

Harvey didn't reply. John smiled.

"There's a job up north next month and we'll need firepower." John sipped his brandy and smacked his lips, a subconscious habit that Harvey had always noticed. "I'll need you and Julios to pick up something for me before then. The less you know, the better. I'll give you details nearer the time. But needless to say, you won't fit a crate of automatic rifles on the back of your bike. So you'll have a van. Sergio will make the arrangements."

Harvey took a breath at the mention of the name; putting his life on the line for a job arranged by Sergio was a risk.

"Sergio?"

"Leave him to me, Son."

"Aren't you concerned at all about the repercussions? Bradley was a major player in the Thomson empire."

"No. I'm not. Leave it to me," replied John.

It was enough to silence Harvey's cynicism. John's short words were a demonstration of his power, which Harvey neither feared nor had the patience to counter.

"A crate of rifles? I can handle that on my own. Why send Julios?"

"In case the job goes south, Harvey. I don't want you there on your own. Sergio will make the arrangements. It's his contacts."

Harvey frowned.

"What's going to happen? Cash in a bag, guns in the van, I check, they check, we both leave. What can go south?"

"It's the *Thomsons*, Harvey," said John, as

he set the knife down and mirrored Harvey's position leaning on the island.

"You're buying *guns* from the *Thomsons*? Correct me if I'm wrong, but didn't Julios and I just off one of their main men and string him up?"

"You did, Harvey. But remember yourself. Don't question me." John often reminded people who he was, regardless of who they were. "Have a little faith in your old man. Think about it. Sergio's faux pas may just work in our favour." John tapped his temple with his index finger. "Right now, Terry Thomson is trying to work out who killed his boy. He probably thinks that whoever did it wanted the Thomsons out of the way for the northern job. Right?"

"Right."

"This gun meet has been lined up for a while now. Why on earth would I put a hit on his son so close to a deal? He knows we don't have the men to go up against him."

"So who's he going to think it was?"

"Who has the men to do the northern job and happens to have a weakness for diamonds?"

"The Stimsons," said Harvey. "This gets

worse. But what we did to Bradley Thomson isn't Stimson's style."

"Yeah. But the Stimsons are the biggest jewel thieves in the country. If anybody is going to go after the northern job, it'll be Adam Stimson. Or Terry Thomson. We aren't even players." John took a swig of his brandy and puckered his lips. "If I'm right, which I normally am, Thomson will come to the same conclusion. He'll go after Stimson."

"Right."

"Which means *we* get the Thomsons and the Stimsons out of the way, *and* we get the guns. The job is ours for the taking, Son."

"So the job is jewels. You're going to start a war and then nick a load of diamonds. What happened to us running bars and doing over cash vans?"

"Slight correction, Harvey. I believe Sergio *already* started the war. I'm just making the best of a bad situation."

Harvey didn't reply.

John tipped the carrots into a saucepan of boiling water and banged the chopping board with the knife.

"You hungry, Harv? This'll be ready in five minutes."

Harvey didn't reply.

"So tell me what you're up to anyway," said John. "Is everything okay?"

"Everything is fine. I want to ask you something."

"Anything for you, Son. Take a seat. Ask away. I'd offer you a drink, but you'd only refuse."

Harvey didn't reply.

"You look like you've got something on your mind, Harvey. What's up?"

"Tell me again about how you found us."

"How what? How I found you? Oh, Harvey. I told you before. You need to drop it, mate."

"I need to hear it again. The small details."

"There *are* no small details, Harvey. You and your sister were left on a seat in my bar in East Ham."

"And my parents? I mean my real parents."

"Harvey, come on. We've been over this how many times?"

"I know. But something doesn't add up. None of it adds up. It never has done."

"You were found with a note from your

mum. I'm sorry, Harvey. I've always hated saying this part. But they both killed themselves. I don't know why. I wish I still had the note. But I didn't know them. I just happened to own the bar nearby, I guess. I was well known, Harvey. Maybe they knew we'd take care of you." John had used that phrase countless times in response to the countless times Harvey had raised the topic. It was verbatim.

"Barb wanted to keep you both," he continued. He spoke slowly as if savouring the memory. "We couldn't have any more kids. You know, complications. We finished up in the bar one night. The staff had all gone home, and we were cleaning up. We did it all ourselves back then. We found you in a little hamper with your sister sitting by your side."

"Wrapped in blankets," finished Harvey.

"Wrapped in blankets," said John in confirmation.

Harvey stood in silence, replaying the scene over in his mind.

"Are we done, Harvey?" said John. "I need a favour."

"I guess we are."

"I need you to shadow Donny."

CHAPTER SEVENTEEN

Harvey found Donny's car tucked into an alleyway behind one of John's bars. He stopped his bike outside a cafe opposite and selected a window seat inside with his back to the wall. He picked up a random newspaper left on a table as he entered, ordered a tea and settled in for the second monotonous day of shadowing his foster brother.

John hadn't issued a specific reason for tailing Donny. He only said that he should keep him in sight and report back with anything he deemed out of the ordinary. But in the sleazy world of fast cars, drugs and cheap women, everything in Donny's life seemed out of the ordinary.

From his seat in the cafe, the view of the bar's entrance was skewed only by passing traffic on foot and on the road. Harvey drank his tea slowly and watched as a contracted cleaning firm entered the bar. Three women armed with buckets, mops and bags of products went inside. Two hours later, they left in their small van. Nobody else walked in. Nobody else walked out.

"Are you going to order something, sweetheart?" said a shrill voice beside Harvey's ear. "It'll be lunchtime soon and the crowds will come in." As she spoke, the door opened and rang the small bell above it. Two tradesmen dressed in grubby jeans entered the cafe.

"Morning, boys," the woman said.

"Alright, Rose? A couple of bacon rolls please, love," said the larger of the two men.

"No problem, darling. Take a seat. I'll be right with you."

She turned to look back at Harvey, who was staring out the window. He felt her gaze and turned to face her.

"What takes the most time to cook?" said Harvey. "I'm waiting for someone. He's late."

"The all-day breakfast," said Rose.

"I'll take one," replied Harvey, already looking back out the window.

"*Please?*" said Rose.

Harvey turned to face her again but didn't say a word.

"One all-day coming up then," she said as she walked off.

One of the things Harvey had learned from Julios was how to communicate without words. Often a mere expression or gesture would convey his thoughts. It was a skill he had never been taught directly, but over time, he had improved it and it became natural. Of course, it was another reflection of Julios' techniques imprinted upon him. As Harvey sat at the table in the small cafe in East Ham staring out of the window, his own reflection stared back at him from the glass. It seemed to question who he was.

To the outside world, Harvey Stone didn't exist. He was a shadow raised by his criminal foster father. He was unknown to the world and trained to be a killer by London's finest hitman. But the reflection saw through his hardened exterior to a time when a young boy, angered by the deaths of his family and frustrated with loneliness, felt the first violent pang of the beast developing in the pit of his stomach.

At first, John had asked Julios to spend time with Harvey to help him mourn. But as time went by, and Julios saw potential in the boy, their training sessions developed from fitness to defence. And then finally, attack.

Julios and Harvey always trained in the large gym to the rear of John's house. The gym was a standard oblong building with a pitched roof and floor-to-ceiling glazing that ran around the perimeter and boasted a view of the wooden deck and swimming pool. It was separated from the main house by a short walk across the lawns.

After training one day, man and boy had walked to the house for some water. Inside, John had been holding a monthly meeting. They were an opportunity for John to demonstrate his power, show off his wealth, and get a feel for the men who were running his various operations.

As Julios and Harvey filled glasses of water in the kitchen, two of the men had walked in behind them. They lit cigarettes and asked the cook for coffee. Then they waited while she boiled water, exchanging whispered comments in each other's ears. Harvey watched them curiously.

The first man took a drag on his cigarette and moved across to the sink to tap away the ash. Leaning on the counter with his back to Harvey and Julios, he continued his hushed conversation with the second man, using wild arm gestures to emphasise his point. As he turned to tap his ash once more and blow smoke up towards the open window, his profile was framed in the sunlight that shone through the glass.

Harvey froze. He instantly recognised the large, crooked nose, the pointed chin and the outline of the man who had haunted his dreams since...

Hannah.

Harvey had seen the face profile before. He'd recognised the movement as the man relaxed his head back to smoke. He'd heard the sound of his breathing.

Only previously, it had been by moonlight.

A crash of crockery on the tiled floor snapped Harvey from his daydream. The two tradesmen slid their chairs across the tiled floor to help Rose pick up the smashed plates. Harvey looked back out the window.

Donny's car hadn't moved. There was no sign of life in the bar, but outside, school children ambled past with their heads buried in mobile phones. They walked in groups of twos and threes and sometimes more, their voices loud and shrill as they called to friends across the street.

But one boy walked past alone. Ignoring stares and deep in his own troubled thoughts, he looked like the weight of the world hung from his shoulders. His head snatched to the left as if he felt Harvey's gaze and the two locked eyes for a brief moment. Then the boy passed out of sight but remained for a while in Harvey's thoughts. He recognised the suffering on the boy's face and was reminded of a time when he too wore the same haunted look.

The outline of the man's face in the sunlight all those years ago had stirred a dark memory in Harvey. It had been as if the sheer will of his conscience had suppressed the image beneath layers of camouflaged emotions. But Julios had picked up on Harvey's mood change with an almost parental instinct.

That afternoon when they were training, he'd stopped and lowered his pads, leaving Harvey poised and ready for the attack.

"That man in the kitchen," began Julios. "You know him?"

Harvey didn't reply.

But a single silent stare from Julios elicited a response.

"What man?" asked Harvey, continuing to hold his guard up and offering no emotion.

Julios was an artist at communicating without words. He was the Da Vinci of facial gestures. He looked down at Harvey with understanding in his eyes.

"I thought he was someone else," Harvey lied.

His eyes diverted to the floor and his guard dropped.

But Julios continued to stare. The urge to blurt it out, to tell Julios, his only living friend, what he'd seen that night was so strong. But he couldn't. It would be weak. Julios wouldn't understand.

Instead, he returned Julios' stare with a look of his own.

Julios nodded.

"I think it is time for patience, planning and execution," Julios had said.

Harvey was dragged back to reality when the waitress cleared her throat.

"Are you going to stay much longer?" she said, staring down at the cold all-day breakfast. "You've been sitting here all day."

Behind her, on the wall above the kitchen door, was a clock. Harvey checked the alleyway.

Donny's car was gone.

He pulled a twenty-pound note from his pocket, which he slammed on the table, then jumped up and pulled on his helmet while walking to his bike. The late afternoon traffic was building up. Harvey glanced left then right, scanning the cars, and for the briefest of moments, he saw the tail end of Donny's Mercedes turning left at the Green Street traffic lights.

CHAPTER EIGHTEEN

"There's someone following us," said Donny, as he pulled off London's North Circular Road. "It's the same beaten-up old wreck we saw in East Ham."

From the passenger seat of Donny's Mercedes, Sergio leaned forward to look into the mirror. But he saw nothing.

"There's nobody, Donny. You're high and paranoid."

"I'm not paranoid, Sergio," spat Donny. A thin layer of sweat had formed on his brow and he chewed his lower lip with his front teeth. "Look. Three cars back."

They stopped at a set of lights with Epping Forest on their left.

"I'm going to turn left and see if they follow," said Donny. "If they do, we'll lose them in the country lanes."

"There's nobody there, Donny. Relax."

The seconds ticked by as the traffic flowed in the opposite direction, but as soon as the lights turned green, Donny floored the big saloon. The rear wheels spun, and the car screeched into the lane where a series of sweeping curves were followed by a long straight.

"Is he there? Did he follow?" said Donny, gripping the wheel and checking the mirror.

Sergio turned in his seat as they emerged from the last bend and Donny found fourth gear.

"I don't see anybody," said Sergio. "See, I told you. There's nothing to worry about."

But as soon as he'd said the words, the rust-coloured heap that Donny had spotted earlier nosed into view and entered the straight. Its body was twisted and its front end raised with the torque of the engine.

"Hold on," said Sergio.

"What?" said Donny, wiping his sweaty hand on his trouser legs. "Tell me what you see."

"It's that old car," said Sergio over the noise of the engine. "He's catching."

"He can't be catching. We're doing seventy miles an hour."

"Go faster, Donny. He's right behind us."

"I'm trying," said Donny.

"Faster, Donny."

Donny's eyes flicked to the mirror and back to the road. But it was too late. The front end of the rust bucket slammed into the rear of the Mercedes. Donny fought with the steering, but the force of the blow had already sent the car swinging from side to side. Sergio gripped the safety handle above the door with one hand and with the other, he held onto the smooth dashboard. As Donny slammed on the brakes, the wheels left the tarmac, found the forest floor, and sent the car into a series of rolls and spins.

Then silence ensued.

Sergio's head smashed the passenger window on the first roll and Donny's face bent into the steering wheel. Then, as the car flipped end to end, a weightless yet hopeless feeling came over the men as their world spun in slow motion. They were thrown around the front of the car. All around was chaos, which was brought to a bone-shattering stop with the aid of a fat tree that stood in the car's path.

Neither man spoke at first. The only sounds were the soft chinks of broken glass falling to the forest floor and the chattering of birds and squirrels in the trees above. And then a footstep on a snapped twig.

"Can you move?" said Donny, holding his broken nose.

"Shh," said Sergio, aware of the blood running from his forehead.

"What is it?"

Donny's red eyes glowed in the semi-darkness.

"Somebody's there," Sergio whispered.

Liquid sloshed inside a metallic container. A lid was being unscrewed. And then the smell of petrol.

"He's going to burn us," said Sergio, as he fought to remove his seat belt. "Get out."

"I can't," said Donny. "My foot is stuck behind the pedals."

"Well pull it out," said Sergio

Oily liquid began to drip into the front of the car.

"Faster, Donny."

"I'm stuck, Sergio."

The rush of flames across the vehicle and pop of air pockets finding heat silenced them both.

"Get *out*, Donny."

Sergio pulled himself through the passenger window, stinging his hands on the searing surface of the car. He dropped to the forest floor and rolled away from the heat as the flames found a puddle of fuel and reached high into the air.

The car was on its side with the driver's door against the ground. Beyond the burning wreck on the tarmac a hundred metres away, the beaten-up old car roared away, a flash of rust between the forested shades of green.

"Sergio," screamed Donny. "Help me."

But Sergio was frozen to the spot. With his back against a tree and his ruined hands clamped around his body, all he could do was sit and watch. Pink fleshy hands beat against the windscreen as Donny strived to break free and find air. He was screaming at Sergio for help. But then the hands dropped. There was stillness. All Sergio could do was bury his head between his arms and let the tears fall as Donny succumbed to the fire.

CHAPTER NINETEEN

Thick billowing smoke poured from the canopy of dense forest, marking the spot. Harvey jumped the red lights, turned into the bend with his knees just inches from the tarmac, and powered up the road. Cutting a straight line through the long, sweeping bends, he entered the straight at high speed, just in time to see the tail end of an old car as it tore away from the scene.

A quick glance at the wreckage as he shot past told him it was serious, giving him just a fraction of a second to make his decision. Catch the car or make sure Donny was safe.

Harvey braked heavily and felt the tail

end of his bike weave from side to side. Then, using the momentum, he opened up the throttle, turned the front wheel, and went into a wild wheel spin in the centre of the road. Once he'd turned one hundred and eighty degrees, he sped back to the crash.

Stopping twenty feet from Donny's car, he pulled off his helmet and searched the area to find Sergio wallowing in a guilt-ridden stupor.

"Where's Donny?" said Harvey

Sergio immediately appeared glad to see Harvey. But there was no need for him to answer. The hope in Sergio's face dropped to dismay as he stared at the burning car.

"He's in the car?" asked Harvey, dropping his helmet and searching through the smoke for a sign of his foster brother. With his jacket pulled up to protect his face from the searing heat, he stepped towards the flames.

"Donny?" he called out and kicked at the upturned roof. "Donny, are you there?"

No answer came at first. But when Harvey was about to move away, a fist punched the windscreen from the inside. The effort was futile, but it was enough to let

Harvey know Donny was alive. The hard sole of Harvey's boot cracked the windscreen on the second kick. The fourth punched a hole, emitting a waft of thick, foul smoke. Finding a broken branch, Harvey wedged it into the gap, hung all of his weight on the end, and levered the sheet of laminated glass from the car.

Flames licked at the fresh fuel and smoke filled the interior space, but Donny's hand reached out.

"I'm stuck," he called, coughing and fighting for air. "My foot is stuck in the pedals."

The fire had found the high side of the car, and the passenger seat had already begun to smoulder, sending hot drips of melted plastic onto Donny, who was powerless to avoid them.

With a single large stride, his knife in hand and his jacket pulled over his face, Harvey forced his leg through the empty window and into the car. He placed his legs on the back seat with his front laying across his foster brother, allowing him to reach down and cut the laces from Donny's leather shoes.

He pulled the foot free just as flames took

the passenger seat and sent black smoke in every direction. Harvey shoved himself through the windscreen, reached back inside, blind in the poisonous fumes, and found Donny. Then with a final haul, he pulled him free and the two men rolled clear of the fire.

But Donny was unconscious.

Harvey dragged him aside, shouting at Sergio to move. Then he leaned Donny against the tree, loosening his clothes and feeling for a pulse.

"Is he alive?" said Sergio, his voice wavering and his eyes wide with fear.

"No thanks to you," Harvey replied. "Call John. *Now*."

Sergio, in his traumatised state, barely spoke two words to John when Harvey ripped the phone from his hands.

"John, I need a car here now. Epping Road. Look for the smoke. Donny's hurt. We'll take him back to your house so get the doctor."

"Is he okay?" asked John.

"He will be. Just get me that car before the police turn up."

"I'm on it now," said John. "What else do you need?"

Harvey scanned the scene. There was no saving the licenses plates. The fire was too intense and Donny's belongings were in the car. The police would trace it for sure.

"I need a body," said Harvey.

CHAPTER TWENTY

"Sir, traffic just flagged a red light being jumped out near Chigwell in Essex," said Mills. "Vehicle is a BMW motorcycle matching the model that fits those tyre tracks."

"Chigwell, you say?" said Frank. "Do we have an ID?"

"Tenant is scanning the BMW database now."

"It's a bit wild, Mills, and unlikely our man would be as careless as that."

"Right now, sir, we need every lead we can get."

Behind Frank's desk was a large pinboard. He turned in his chair to face the photos he'd pinned up on it. John Cartwright was on one side, along with all known accomplices. Terry Thomson was on the other side with his usual suspects. Below, Frank had left a space for Adam Stimson. There was no photo, just a placeholder with an avatar.

"Do you really think it's Stimson, sir?" asked Mills.

"You want the truth, Mills?" he replied. "I really don't know this time."

"Maybe we'll actually get to see his face if it is."

"You should go home, Mills," said Frank. "You don't need to wait for me. Why don't you go and have a drink with the others?"

"Are you kicking me out, sir?"

"No, Mills. No. But you work hard enough," said Frank. His Scottish accent had lost its subtlety. He checked his watch. "Would you look at that? It's passed seven o'clock already."

"I'd rather stay and make some progress, sir," said Mills. "I've just got the database report from Tenant."

"Anything of interest?" replied Frank, staring hard at the black-and-white photo of Terry Thomson.

"Hold on," she replied.

Frank turned back to her. He knew the look on her face. He'd seen it a dozen times before, and with that look on her face, the girl was always right.

"You've found something?"

"It's just a name, sir. All the details are fake. His address, date of birth and national insurance number all belong to someone else."

"How do you know?"

Frank pulled open the bottom drawer of his desk and produced a small bottle of scotch and two glasses.

"Not for me, sir, thanks," said Melody.

Frank poured one for himself and watched his prodigy scan through the files on her laptop screen.

"Well for one, sir, he's dead."

"Who's dead?"

"The man who owns the motorcycle," said Melody. "He died four years ago."

"How?" asked Frank.

But the flow of conversation was broken by the ringing of her mobile phone.

"Mills," she answered, a little too abruptly.

A female voice spoke with a soft tone, but

that was all Frank could make out. He turned and faced his pinboard while Melody took the call, imagining a link between the three families in front of him and rolling the glass of scotch between his fingers and thumb.

"Thank you," said Mills.

As soon as she put down her phone, the tapping of laptop keys resumed. Frank waited. He knew there would be news, but the trick with somebody as keen as Mills was to let them articulate it in their own time, rather than extract information through questions before they were ready.

"Sir, there's been an incident. It could be relevant."

It was a polite way to ask Frank to turn and face her. So he did. Mills placed the laptop on the desk so they could both see the screen. It showed an internet map of Essex with the M25 circling the city and thick patches of green depicting Epping Forest.

Using a pen, Mills indicated an area of road between Chigwell and Epping.

"This is Epping Road, sir," she said.

"Epping Road?" said Frank. His attention had been captured.

"Police just found a burned-out car there."

"So?"

"The car belonged to Donald Cartwright."

"Was it a crash?" asked Frank.

Mills nodded.

"It's over a hundred metres into the forest and laying on its side. He must have been travelling at speed."

"Is there..." began Frank. But he hesitated.

"A body? One, sir. Burned beyond recognition. All the local police know is that it's a male and the size and height match Donald Cartwright's description."

Frank turned back to his wall and started up at Terry Thomson.

"You couldn't just wait, could you?" he muttered.

"Sorry, sir?"

"Nothing."

Frank downed the remainder of his drink. He pushed himself out of his chair and reached for a red marker on his desk. Then, careful to keep the lines straight and neat, he drew a cross from corner to corner on Donny Cartwright's photograph.

"What does that tell you?" he asked Melody.

Her eyes flicked from side to side then to the avatar placeholder representing Stimson.

"Balance, sir."

"Nicely put," Frank remarked. "So we have Bradley Thomson dead. And our suspects are Cartwright or Stimson-"

"And now we have Donny Cartwright dead," said Melody. "And our suspects are-"

"Thomson and Stimson," Frank finished. "So either the Cartwrights and the Thomsons are at each other's throats, or Stimson really is starting a war."

"There's one more thing, sir," said Melody. She waited for him to glance back over his shoulder then pointed at her laptop. Using the pen again, she indicated a small area of the road. "This junction here."

"Yes?" said Frank.

"This is where the motorbike jumped the lights."

"The dead guy," said Frank. "Who was he?"

"Well that's the interesting thing, sir," said Melody. "His name was Albert Small."

"It doesn't ring a bell," said Frank. "Should it?"

"He was found buried in a shallow grave four years ago deep inside Epping Forest."

"He was murdered?" said Frank, reaching for the bottle.

"Pathologist reports say he was buried alive."

Cogs began to fall into place in Frank's mind. But Mills hadn't finished.

"He'd just been released from Belmarsh Prison after serving seven years for aggravated sexual assault on several girls."

"He was-"

"A sex offender, sir," finished Mills. "He was one of the unsolved murders."

CHAPTER TWENTY-ONE

A gold bracelet and heavy watch were all that could be seen of John Cartwright's hands, which were forced deep into his pockets in agitation as his son lay on the bed in his old bedroom with an oxygen mask strapped to his face.

"Who did this, Harvey?" John turned at the end of his pace across the room then began again. "Was it Thomson's lot?"

"Never seen him before," said Harvey.

"So you got a look at him?"

"I got close, but not close enough."

"But you *saw* him? You could have got him?"

"From a distance. But I had to stop and

turn back. I *could* have caught him and he *could* be strung up downstairs right now waiting to have his skin peeled off. But then we wouldn't be sitting here waiting for Donny to wake up, would we?"

The statement silenced John. From the corner of Harvey's eye, he saw Sergio shrink further into the chair beside Donny's bed. John caught it too; he glared briefly at Sergio in a demonstration of control then looked away.

"The body was a good idea, Harvey. It'll be at least a week before they realise it's not Donny."

"And when they do?" asked Harvey.

"By the time they realise it was just a lowlife scumbag who can't pay his debts, they'll have a whole new bunch of bodies to be sifting through."

John offered Harvey a wink just as Sergio jumped into life.

"He's moving. I felt his hand. He moved."

"Get the doctor," said John. "He's downstairs."

Sergio ran from the room, calling out for the doctor to come quickly. John leaned over

Donny. With a rarely gentle hand, he brushed Donny's hair from his brow.

"Are you awake, Son?" he asked.

The searing hot metal had singed the side of Donny's face. The bandage was concealing one of his eyes. But the other opened slowly as if for the first time.

"That's my boy," said John. "Don't you move. You're alright. You just had a nasty accident, that's all."

The eye flicked around the room then settled on Harvey and moistened.

"Harvey, over here, before Sergio gets back," said John in his best conspiratorial whisper. "What happened?" he asked Donny. "Was it one of Thomson's lot? I need to know."

A single blink, long but meaningful.

"So you didn't get a look?" asked John. "At the driver? Did you see the driver?"

Donny's swollen lips parted like great cracks in the earth's crust. His tongue slid from his mouth but failed to bring moisture and retreated back inside.

"No," said Donny. His voice was more of a croak than a word, and his efforts fogged the oxygen mask in an instant.

"Don't talk, Donny," said John. "Don't worry. We'll get them. We just need a plan."

"What about the meet?" asked Harvey. "Is it still on?"

With both hands resting on the bed, John turned his head sideways to face Harvey and nodded.

"The gun deal is still on. Nothing changes."

Donny became restless. His legs twitched, and he tried to speak.

"Easy, Son," said John. "Just take it easy."

Using his forearm, Donny tried to pull the mask from his face, but only managed to push to it one side.

"The northern job," he croaked.

John repositioned the mask over Donny's mouth just as the doctor entered the room. Sergio walked in behind him, pleased that he'd been able to help.

"It's still on," said John, looking between his two sons. "Nothing changes."

The doctor began to assess Donny's condition, ordering Sergio to refill the water jug. The reprise offered John a chance to pull Harvey to one side.

But Harvey spoke first.

"You just lost a man for the northern job. Don't ask me."

The stare John returned was understanding yet frustrated. He knew not to push Harvey.

"Now Thomson and Stimson will think that Donny is dead. If it was Stimson who did this, he'll be under the impression that neither the Thomsons nor us can do the job. We'll be too busy mourning."

"What if it was Thomson?" asked Harvey.

"Well, I guess we'll find out when you and Julios go and collect our guns, won't we?"

"We need to make sure they think Donny is dead. We need them both to think that we're out of the game for a while."

"I'll be back tomorrow," said the doctor with a raised voice to cut into the whispered conversation. He had his bag in his hand and was ready to leave. "He's stable, but his wounds will need cleaning and dressing twice daily."

"Thanks, doctor," said John. "I really appreciate you coming, and, of course-"

"You've known me long enough to know I won't talk, John." The doctor leaned forward, met John's eyes and spoke with the serious hushed tones of a surgeon practised at delivering bad news. "He'll be scarred for life. His hands will heal but the side of his face won't, I'm afraid."

"Understood," said John, nodding and staring at Sergio, who stood doting over Donny.

The doctor brushed past them but turned back at the door. "Make sure you keep him hydrated and call me if there's any change."

"What about a bit of sunshine and saltwater?" asked John.

"I don't follow," replied the doctor.

"Would it do him any good relaxing by the sea?"

The doctor nodded.

"Yes. In a week or so, maybe."

"Thanks, doctor. I'll call if there's anything else."

Harvey and John moved to Donny's side. Sergio sensed the change in atmosphere and fell back into the seat. John removed the oxygen mask. The examination had woken Donny, and his eye waited for John to speak.

"Sergio," began John, "I want you to

arrange a holiday for Donny. Somewhere hot. The Maldives, maybe?"

"But, Dad, what about the northern job?" Donny's voice was still cracked and broken but was clearer than it had been.

"Once you've done that, Sergio," continued John, ignoring his son's question, "I want you to arrange a funeral."

"Whose funeral?" croaked Donny.

John smiled the smile of a man who had a plan and would go any length to see it through.

"Yours, Son."

John's gaze switched between his two sons.

"But don't worry. It'll be an event to remember. We'll all be deeply sad. Won't we, Harvey?"

Harvey didn't reply.

CHAPTER TWENTY-TWO

"Morning, boys," said Terry as he entered his office. "I suppose you heard the good news?"

"What's that, boss?" asked Rob, removing his feet from the coffee table.

"Poor old Donny Cartwright was involved in a nasty accident. I hear it was fatal," said Terry. "Terrible shame."

"Old John Cartwright must be in a right old state," said Lenny, flicking the page of his newspaper.

"I hope so," said Terry, the joy lost from his voice. "Where's the nonce?"

"In his room, boss. I think he's saying goodbye to his testicles."

"Well, get him out here. I need to go over tomorrow's plan with you all."

The two men exchanged glances. In Terry's mind, they were both equal. But between them, an unofficial rank elevated Lenny above Rob. He had worked for Terry for a longer period and therefore been involved in more jobs. Rob stood to leave the room.

"Get me a tea while you're up, Rob, will you?" said Terry.

"I wouldn't say no to a tea, come to think of it, Rob. Cheers, mate," said Lenny.

Rob left the room with an audible sigh. He returned a few minutes later with a sheepish-looking Shaun in tow.

"Take a seat, Shaun," said Terry. Shaun did as he was told and sat at the desk where Terry had broken him and reduced him to a snivelling wreck. "No. Not there. Let's join Lenny on the couches. I need to talk to you all, and I don't want to shout across the room."

Shaun stood and distanced himself by taking the furthest seat from Lenny. A few moments later, Rob returned, carrying a tray with three teas and a little plate of biscuits.

"Shaun, do you want a tea, mate?" asked Terry.

"Erm..." Shaun hesitated. His eyes flicked to the tray of steaming teas and cold cookies.

"Get Shaun a tea, will you, Rob? While you're up."

"*Him?*" answered Rob. "Tea?"

"We're going to have a civilised chat and Shaun's one of us now. So he needs a cup of tea. You've got a tea. Lenny's got a tea. I've got a tea. Shaun needs a tea, and seeing as you clearly possess the tea-making skills in this band of merry men, you have my vote for tea maker of the year. The man of the hour goes to you. Now go and make Shaun a tea."

"Cracking tea, Rob," said Lenny, sipping at one of the mugs.

Rob turned to return to the kitchen, muttering to himself.

"Hold on, Rob," said Terry. "Shaun, how do you like it?"

At the mention of his name, Shaun looked up, slightly embarrassed but enjoying the banter.

"Like it?"

"Tea, Shaun. Tea."

"Oh, tea. White, please."

"White," said Rob.

"You want sugar, Shaun?" asked Terry.

"Have a sugar, Shaun," said Lenny.

"One please, Rob," said Shaun, doing his best not to smirk.

"So, let's get this straight. One cup of steaming-hot tea, white with one sugar," summarised Terry. "You got that, Rob?"

"It's not rocket science, boss," said Rob, trying to sound cheerful and not let the banter get the better of him.

He walked away.

"The British Empire was forged on good tea, Rob. Just remember that," called Terry.

"Yeah, I know," said Rob, as he reached the door. "I remember the time Alfred the Great stopped killing all the Vikings and made them tea instead. They all stopped fighting, sat down, and had a nice brew and a chat. Then the big ugly Viking pulled his great big sword out of the big ugly Englishman and produced a packet of bourbons from his pocket."

"That might be taking it a bit too far, Rob," said Lenny.

"Yeah, a bit far that, Rob," said Terry. "Vikings used to like custard creams, mate, not chocolate bourbons."

Lenny and Terry chuckled to themselves

while Rob shook his head and walked away. He returned a few moments later with one more cup of tea, which he placed on the coffee table in front of Shaun.

"Thank you, Rob."

"Right, now that we've all got tea, finally, can we discuss the job tomorrow?" said Terry. "The meet is at six o'clock, and I trust you've been to check the place out." He looked at Lenny questioningly.

"Yeah, not a problem, boss," replied Lenny.

"Good. You'll be meeting Cartwright's boys and they'll be fired up. So be on guard. Shaun, you are our number one. You will be on your own. Lenny and Rob won't be far away, but you can manage it. You won't need them."

"On my own?" blurted Shaun. "But-"

"Don't worry. Lenny and Rob will be close by to make sure nothing happens."

"Why *me?* I don't know anything about it. I don't even know *what* it is we're doing."

"Well, in that garage over there is a big box of guns, Shaun. When we're done talking, you three are going to load them all into the van. Then tomorrow, you're going to take them up to a cosy little spot in the pretty English countryside. You're going to sit, wait, and then sell them to the men that arrive at six o'clock."

"*Guns?* You want me to sell guns? But-"

"But what, Shaun? You could be sitting in a cell in prison. You *could* get eaten by pigs too, and you've managed to avoid that so far. But by the skin of your balls, I might add. It's easy. They rock up. You show them the guns. They nod their heads, give you the cash before they put the box in their own van, and you drive off."

"This is serious stuff. I don't know."

"Shaun, Shaun, Shaun. Calm down," said Terry. "Lenny?"

"Boss?"

"What would you rather, given a choice? Go to prison for selling guns to villains? Or go to prison for letting underage girls lick your lollipop?"

"Selling guns, boss. I imagine I'd have a much nicer time." Lenny continued to dunk his biscuit into his tea as he spoke.

"There you go, Shaun. See, we've given you options, son. If you were walking free now, waiting for your court date, you would have probably been lynched by the locals. Then you would have gone to prison as a nonce, and you'd have more fingers in you than a bucket of KFC. But now, you have options. You *could* always turn yourself in. Or you can do this job for me as a thanks. Yes, there is a small risk of getting caught and going to prison. But at least it won't be for dirty sex offences. Failing that, the pigs are hungry. So there are three options on the table, Shaun. You, mate, are a very lucky boy."

"What if they want to take the guns before they pay me the money? How am I going to stop them?"

"Just close the van doors, Shaun. Get in and drive off," said Lenny.

"If they want them that bad, and they do, I know they do, they'll soon hand over the cash," said Terry. "Done right, the deal will take fifteen minutes, tops."

"And do I go free after?"

"Free?" cried Terry. "Free? Shaun, you are free. I just told you. I should mention that you have now skipped bail and are wanted by the police, but you are *definitely* free to go."

Terry picked up his tea, dunked a biscuit, and took a bite.

"After the job, what then?"

"We'll see, Shaun," said Terry, swallowing his biscuit. "I could do with another pair of hands. Maybe we'll keep you on." He popped the other half of the biscuit into his mouth. "Clive on the farm needs help with the pigs. Maybe you could be his farmhand if the pigs don't mind the smell. We'll talk about that when you get back."

"Can I ask one more question, please?" Shaun sat forward, put his own tea on the table, and folded his hands. "How come I'm going to be on my own?"

Terry put down his tea, sat forward, and mimicked Shaun by folding his hands. "The men we are selling the guns to are-" Terry searched for the right words. "A little upset right now. They'll be a bit jumpy. And when men like that are jumpy, it can get dangerous."

"Dangerous?"

"These are very serious men, Shaun. They are the sneakiest, most cunning, and deviant villains I know, and I happen to know a lot of villains. It would not surprise me in the slightest if they shoot you dead and take the guns. That's why Lenny and Rob will be close by, to make sure they don't get away without paying one way or another."

Shaun sat back. "So I'm..."

"Expendable, Shaun. Expendable is what you are."

CHAPTER TWENTY-THREE

In a coffee shop on a small side road off Epping High Street, Harvey sat at a corner table with his back to the wall. He was waiting for Julios to arrive to discuss their plans. The location of their meets always varied. It was a stipulation of Julios to avoid regular patterns.

The tables inside the coffee shop were empty. Rush hour had been and gone, and the few customers that did come through the door ordered takeouts.

A few minutes passed before Julios' old Subaru drove past the first time. Harvey counted down from sixty, picturing Julios performing his routine check of the surroundings before the car passed by once more and parked facing the fastest way out of town. Julios ambled into the coffee shop as if time would wait for him, noting every person in sight with a discreet flick of his eyes. Constant voyeurism was another of Julios' habits born from years of looking over his shoulder.

The big man stepped up to the door wearing his long overcoat, thick pants and boots. He ignored the welcoming smile of the waitress and took a seat on the table next to Harvey's, also facing the door with his back to the wall.

They both ordered coffee, which was delivered with effortless manners and minimal disturbance. Menus were placed in front of the two men, but the waitress didn't offer the special of the day or push for a food order. Instead, she left her only two customers to talk in near silence, their gestures filling the gaps between their sparse words.

"They got to Donny," said Harvey.

A frown formed on Julios' brow.

"Either Thomson or Stimson. I didn't get a look," Harvey continued. "Donny's in a bad way and John is mad as hell. He's sending him away and faking the funeral. Give it six months and he'll be back with a new identity."

A sideways stare from Julios asked another silent question before his eyes returned to monitoring the traffic outside.

"I think it was Thomson. An act of revenge."

Julios nodded.

"Which makes tomorrow's deal slightly more complex," said Harvey.

The statement caught Julios' attention.

"But it's still on. John sent me the location," said Harvey.

Julios considered the response then nodded and raised an eyebrow in another silent question.

"It's a safe enough spot. In a small grass clearing along a country lane in the sticks," said Harvey. "I checked it all out."

But Julios' face remained the same. The question hadn't been fully answered.

"It looks like a turning space for tractors and farm machinery. It's no bigger than required, just enough for two vans to pull up side by side. It's protected from the road by big hedges, and it's one minute to the M11 motorway at high speed."

Harvey took a sip of his coffee before he continued.

"There are thick trees on three sides of the location. We'll need to be there first to do a recce and see anybody coming. So there's no real chance of an ambush."

A slight nod from Julios was enough to confirm his approval. He didn't need the details but just certainty that Harvey had done the research. Julios trusted Harvey's word. He believed that it was a safe place, and all risks were known.

"Sergio has arranged a van. Meet me at John's tomorrow morning. Given the circumstances, we'll travel separately. I'll take my bike. You take the van."

Julios gave another nod as he sipped at his coffee then placed the cup on the table. He played with the handle distractedly. It was unusual behaviour for Julios. Something was on his mind. The big man was sitting motionless. A soft grumbling sound from the back of his throat was the only sign he was about to speak.

"Do you remember your first time?" asked Julios. His voice was cracked and hoarse, more from the lack of use than anything else. "The first time you killed?"

"I remember," said Harvey, nodding. "The boy in the woods."

"No, no, no," said Julios, his face screwing with distaste. "That was not a kill. That was you and your immaturity letting your emotions run away. It was anger in its purest form, seeking something that you'd never find. When I ask you if you remember your first kill, I'm asking about the first time I showed you. The first time you felt control. The first time you fed the beast inside you."

"Yes," said Harvey.

"I remember it also. Very well in fact," continued Julios. He gazed across the cafe in wistful thought. "I remember it as clearly as I remember my own first time. I watched from the shadows as Jack came home from one of John's meetings. I could see the light in your eyes. They were like two sharp diamonds in a soft blanket of shadow. Jack poured himself a drink and lit the small lamp beside the record player when you stepped out behind him. I urged you to get back, to wait. It wasn't time. But still, you stayed there. You seemed to take delight in his ignorance."

"There's not a day that goes past when I don't remember that, Julios," said Harvey.

"I thought he would catch you before you made your move. You stood too long." Julios laughed, singular and nasal, recalling the memory. "And as the music began, powerful and so full of life, Jack lay his head back as he so often did. You bent to one knee, sliced his Achilles then stepped aside to let your prey fall to the floor."

"He was taller than me. I had to get him down to my level."

"I've never seen a boy hold a knife the way you did that night, Harvey. As wrong as it was, I have never felt so proud."

"I needed to do it, Julios. I did it for Hannah."

"You needed to do it, Harvey, so you could continue with your life. You needed to do it so you could enjoy the blissful memories of her. And you needed to do it to feed your inner beast."

"I've been feeding it since," said Harvey.

A smiling exhale from Julios was more of a breath than a laugh.

"Yes, Harvey." He paused. "But your targets, those men you seek, they will never satisfy the hunger."

The two men shared a moment of silence. Harvey hadn't heard Julios speak so much for a long time. He took a deep breath and hung his head forward.

"I have these dreams. I can't sleep for weeks. My targets, my hunt for them, it's the only thing that helps."

"You will not find retribution in that way," said Julios. "You may feed your beast, but he'll just get hungrier. You need to find the man you've been looking for."

"The second man," whispered Harvey. Hate rose up like bile in his throat. He shook his head. "And until then?"

"When you killed Jack. When that boy sank his knife into Jack's eye, a part of you lived. A part of you rejoiced. Find that again, Harvey," said Julios. "Don't let the hunt for retribution take everything from you. Life will pass you by."

His striking dark eyes latched onto Harvey's. They felt as strong as the man's hands, and they wouldn't let go.

"Don't waste your time killing meaningless men, Harvey. Find the other man who attacked Hannah. Allow yourself true revenge. Give the beast its final meal. Then move on with your life."

CHAPTER TWENTY-FOUR

The Automated Number Plate Recognition system used by the Essex police had flagged the motorcycle in less than twenty-four hours from when Mills had submitted the request. A series of emails and calls woke Frank at seven in the morning. By quarter past, he was in his car. By nine o'clock, he was cruising Epping High Street observing every motorcycle he passed, either parked or moving.

It was a small town, so the search didn't take long. When the suspect emerged from a cafe, Frank laid eyes on what could be the biggest catch of his career. If he could tie this vigilante with Bradley's murder, *and* put away

Thomson or Cartwright, it would be like winning the lottery.

But what Frank hadn't counted on was the other man who emerged from the cafe about a minute later. Frank reached for the Nikon DSLR camera he kept in his glove box. Then he snapped three shots of Julios Saville getting into an old Subaru.

The motorbike passed, riding slowly down the narrow street. Frank indicated and pulled out into the road behind him. Maintaining a steady distance, Frank settled in for the tail. He accelerated as any normal driver would with a clear path ahead. Following a small bend beneath a railway bridge, he found himself on a wide country B-road. The suspect was in front by three hundred yards. There was no other traffic in sight.

He slowed.

The bike slowed too, turning right at a roundabout toward Stapleford Abbots.

Frank slowed further and dropped into third gear.

The bike pulled to the side of the road. Seeing no alternative, Frank eased to a stop twenty metres behind him. But the rider didn't move. He made no attempt to dismount or even turn to look at Frank. Instead, he just stared into his mirror.

With slow, deliberate movements, Frank reached for the door handle. The two men locked eyes in the reflection of the bike's mirror. Through the darkened helmet visor, Frank felt the burn of the man's stare.

The door clicked open.

Frank had committed. He lowered his foot onto the tarmac and pulled himself outside. The rider didn't flinch.

"Excuse me," said Frank. He kept one foot inside the car and used the door as protection in case the man turned to shoot at him. "I'm looking for Theydon Bois. Can you tell me where it is, please?"

But the rider didn't move. It was as if he hadn't even heard Frank's voice.

"Did you hear me?" called Frank. "I said I'm looking for Theydon Bois."

He leaned back into the car and reached for his phone. But as he did, without warning, the Subaru roared past, ripping the door from Frank's car with an explosion of twisting metal. Diving for cover and pulling his legs inside, Frank sprawled across the seats, cowering with fear, until the riot of noise had ceased and the whine of the motorcycle faded to nothing.

The car door finished its dizzying spin on the tarmac a hundred yards up the road as Frank pulled himself from the car. Dizzied and shaking from shock, he worked his way to the grass verge then emptied the burning acid contents of his stomach onto the ground.

A few minutes passed, allowing time for Frank's heart to settle, the perspiration to dry and his head to stop spinning. But as he climbed back into his car, he reached for the non-existent door and found only air where it used to be. With his seat belt in place, he indicated then pulled out onto the empty road. The wind whistled past his ear and whipped at his stained trouser leg. He rolled the scene over and over in his mind like a bad dream.

It had been an attack.

"Do they know who I am?"

He was so far behind both the bike and the car that giving chase would have been futile. So he cruised along at well below the speed limit while a plan formulated in his head and his shaking hands gripped the steering wheel.

The River Roding ran alongside the road.

It was slow-moving with patches of long reeds dotted by fishermen. Collected beside a small weir, they enjoyed their own version of quiet time. He saw the gleeful arch of a fishing rod. One man stood on the river bank playing his catch. Frank turned in his seat to glance at the action as he passed. He was quietly pleased for the man.

Then he returned his attention to the road ahead, just in time to feel the silence that ensues before death lifts its head and marks a man's mortality with one foul sweep of its cruel hand. It was at that moment that Frank's entire world slowed to a crawl. It was as if he was falling from a cliff, but no matter how hard he tried to hold on, no matter what memory passed through his mind, of love, of life, of winning and losing, he couldn't help but fall.

The Subaru entered his peripheral vision.

Frank saw the spot where the two cars would collide.

He closed his eyes and remembered life.

He thought of love.

He had time for one last breath before the old Subaru slammed into the side of his Volvo.

CHAPTER TWENTY-FIVE

A regular beeping somewhere far away became part of Frank's dream. It grew louder as consciousness weaved its way towards the daylight behind his closed eyes. Slowly opening his lids, Frank saw two nurses standing with their backs to him. Through the open door was a corridor with a lime-green floor and white walls.

The beeping was coming from behind his head. He turned to see it. But a sharp pain rose up like the tail of a scorpion and stung his neck muscles before scurrying away, leaving Frank to groan in pain.

"Mr Carver," said one of the nurses, a

pretty redhead with a light blue uniform and professional smile. "How are you feeling?"

"A little confused if I'm honest," Frank replied.

"You've been in an accident, Mr Carver."

"Call me Frank."

"Okay. You've been in an accident, Frank. You're in St Margaret's Hospital in Epping. Are you in any pain?"

"No," he said, although he was conscious not to move his head.

"There are no broken bones, but you do have severe bruising. So we're going to keep you in for a while."

"What about the other guy?"

"What other guy, Frank? You were travelling alone."

"The other car," said Frank. "The one that hit me?"

"I can find out for you. But as far as I know, you veered off the road, rolled and landed in the river. Two fishermen pulled you out."

"There was another car."

"It's okay, Frank. You've had a nasty hit to your head. Just rest a while and if you need anything, you can press this button here." She showed Frank the little red button on a wire fixed to the side of the bed. Then she left the room, leaving Frank to admire her rear at it swayed from side to side. But the pleasure was short-lived as Melody Mills stepped into view wearing a surprised but friendly smile.

"She's old enough to be your daughter, sir," said Mills.

"I wasn't-"

"It's okay, sir," she said. "I'm sure you're in a lot of shock and not quite yourself."

She placed a small sports bag on the floor and put a smartphone on the bedside table.

"Your replacement phone," said Mills. "I've had Tenant restore a backup. It should look and feel exactly like your last one, minus any messages you received since the last backup."

"Thank you, Mills," said Frank. "How did you know-"

"In case you've forgotten, sir, we work for the UK's finest. We were alerted as soon as your car's number plate was entered into the system."

"Good work." Frank paused. "No grapes?"

"No grapes, I'm afraid. I didn't take you for the grape type, sir. But you'll find a change of clothes in the bag. I had to guess your size so sorry if it's wrong."

"Thank you, Mills," said Frank. "I'm sure they will be fine."

"Is there anything else, sir? What were you doing out here?"

"My car?" said Frank, ignoring her second question.

"It's being pulled from the river and from what I hear, it's a write-off."

"My camera. Can you get my camera?"

"If it was inside, I think you'll be needing a new one, sir."

"See if Tenant can get the photos from it. Keep it confidential. The last few photos are of a man. Run some facial recognition and send me the results."

"I'll see what I can do, sir."

"Thanks," said Frank.

"Oh, before I forget," said Mills, placing a car key beside Frank's new phone. "Black Range Rover in the car park."

"A Range Rover?"

"We figured you needed an upgrade, sir. Denver managed to wrangle it from the carpool. I've put a parking sticker inside so you're good for two days. I'll be back before then to see how you're getting on."

"Thanks, Mills. What would I do without you?"

"Aside from walk home in a hospital gown?" said Mills. "I'll let you rest. But call me if you need anything."

"I need your weapon," said Frank.

"Sir?"

"I was forced off the road, Mills. They might come back for me."

"But, sir, the report says you came off the road and rolled. There was no-one else involved."

"I was there, Mills. I saw the car. It was a Subaru."

"Sir-"

"Just trust me, Mills. Leave your weapon."

All humour dropped as the two locked eyes. Then Mills released her weapon from beneath her armpit, checked behind her for nurses, and tucked it beneath the pile of new clothes in the sports bag.

"Does this have something to do with the camera, sir?"

"Run the facial recognition, Mills. It's important."

"I'm all over it, sir," replied Mills. She made to leave then turned at the door, smiling. "Oh and leave those nurses alone."

The door closed behind her, allowing Frank a moment's peace. But his active mind was already piecing together a plan.

A dull pain seized his arm as he pulled the hydration drip free. A trickle of thin blood ran down his skin, but he wiped it away with his gown before pulling on the fresh t-shirt and trousers. Mills had done a good job guessing his size. Even the shoes were a perfect fit.

His body revolted against the movement. His bruises announced their presence with every effort, and each time, the warnings of his body slowed Frank. But by the time he was dressed and had tucked Mills' weapon into his waistband, he felt he could pass as a visitor. He glanced around the small room, collected his phone, car key and wallet, which was still damp, and eased the door open.

Nurses flitted from room to room in an endless state of controlled hurry. Seeing the reception to his right, Frank slipped into the corridor, walking slowly to minimise the limp from the bruise on his right leg.

As he walked, he diverted his eyes to his phone, trying to avoid the guilty look of a man escaping from prison. He saw the automatic doors ahead. Each second, he waited for a gentle tap on his shoulder or the sound of his name being called out.

Outside was damp. The sky was a dull grey blanket of cloud that filled the space from horizon to horizon. The rain had left a sheen across the surface of the ground. In the corner of the car park, standing alone with an almost conspicuous appearance, was the Range Rover.

Climbing into the car was tougher than Frank had anticipated. Raising his leg aggravated his bruises and the effort to haul himself inside sent stabs of pain through his neck. By the time he was sitting in the seat, he was breathless and questioning his own plan.

Searching his phone, Frank retrieved the message from Terry Thomson with the location of the gun drop. Thankfully, it hadn't been lost. Then he typed a message to Mills stating a fake plan. His finger hovered over the send button. But the intricate lies and tangled web of deceit bore more implications that his imagination could process.

He hit delete.

CHAPTER TWENTY-SIX

Anxiety gripped Shaun's chest with its strong claws the moment he opened his eyes and recognised the small room. He dressed in the only clothes he had, baulking at the smell, and wandered outside. Through the door to Terry's office, Shaun heard three voices. Instead of walking inside, Shaun ventured back to the kitchen, made four cups of tea and found an old tray on which to carry them.

He knocked and walked into the office to find all three men standing around Terry's desk. They looked up as he entered.

"Tea?" he said, hopeful that the gesture would initiate a positive start to the day.

"Now that's what I call cognitive thinking.

Well done, Shaun," said Terry. He appeared to be forcing a jovial mood, masking the lingering sadness for the loss of his son.

"Where should I put them?" he asked.

Lenny reached out, took a cup and passed it to the old man before reaching back and taking one for himself. Rob took one too and left Shaun holding the tray with both hands, unable to let go and remove his own cup. His nerves began to kick in. His hands began to shake and tea spilt onto the tray.

"Stick it on the table over there, Shaun," Lenny said.

The opportunity for a barrage of insults was open, but neither Terry nor Lenny took it. But Rob turned, staring at Shaun while sipping his tea.

"What do *you* want?"

"I...I thought we were planning," replied Shaun, realising he may have intruded.

"Yeah, *we* are planning, but *you* don't need to plan. All you need to do is-"

"Easy, Robby. The bloke just made you a cup of tea. Play nicely," said Terry. "Shaun, squeeze in, mate. You're going to need to know this more than any of us, anyway."

Shaun moved to an empty space around the table where a large map was opened out.

"Right. The drop is at six o'clock. Lenny, talk me through the sequence of events."

"We'll arrive just before six. Rob and me will get out and walk through these trees here." He pointed at the thick line of trees that surrounded the location on three sides. "Just in case Cartwright's lot are planning an ambush. Shaun will take the van in on his own. Rob and I will find-"

"Rob and I, Lenny. It's Rob and I," said Terry.

"Rob and you, boss?" said Lenny.

"No, it's English, Lenny. It's not Rob and *me*. It's Rob and *I*."

"Right. Okay. So Rob and I will find somewhere out of sight to keep an eye on things. If things go well, Shaun will drop the guns and get the money, and we'll be waiting on the road when he pulls out."

"What if things don't go well?"

"Rob and...*I* will be in a good place to step in and take them out. We won't start shooting unless it looks like they're pulling one over on us," finished Lenny.

"Shaun, talk me through it," said Terry, moving his attention to the wiry, nervous kid.

"I'll drop Rob and Lenny off before the car park and then drive in alone."

"Good. Then what?"

"I'll turn the van around so I'm facing the exit as Lenny told me to."

"Good."

"Then I'll wait for them."

"Okay. What happens if a nosy policeman comes sniffing around?"

"I'll tell him that I'm a delivery driver and I just stopped for a break or something."

"Have you got your driver's license on you?"

"Yeah, it's..."

Shaun reached for his wallet in his pocket and removed his license. Lenny took it from him, snapped it in half and tossed the two halves in the waste bin behind Terry.

"Don't be stupid, Shaun. You're all over the news. You're on the run," said Lenny.

"Lenny's right, Shaun. You show a copper that licence and not only will you be nicked for being the dirty, little nonce you are, but they'll also be slapping a fair chunk of time on you for what's in the back of the van." The old man opened the desk drawer to his right and pulled out a wallet. "*This* is your wallet. Throw the other one away."

Shaun opened his wallet again and began to search inside, but Lenny took it from him and tossed it in the bin with the license. He then took the new wallet from Terry and passed it to Shaun.

"So, you're all parked up, and they're there. Now what?"

"I show them the crate?"

"Exactly. Open the doors and step back. Let them work it out. You want to know why?"

"Why?"

"Because, Shaun, if I wanted a load of guns and didn't want to pay, and if the dopey bloke I was buying them off climbed into the back of the van of his own volition, I'd shut the doors on him, drive off and have the lot for nothing. They'd have the van, the money *and* the guns, Shaun."

"Right."

"Then what?"

"They open the crate, have a look, give me the money then move the guns."

"Good boy, Shaun."

"Any questions?"

"No."

"Good. One more thing. Lenny, Rob, I've arranged to have a little bit of security attend. He won't get involved, but he will sit and watch. Don't do anything stupid. Just do what you have to do and everything will be fine," said Terry. "Shaun?"

"Yeah?"

"Don't yeah me, Shaun."

"Sorry."

"I've got a little surprise lined up for the Cartwrights. As soon as the deal is done, you need to get your pervy little backside out of there and don't look back."

"A surprise?" said Shaun. "What kind of surprise?"

"Oink oink, Shaun," said Terry. "Oink oink."

CHAPTER TWENTY-SEVEN

Two hundred yards from the drop, Harvey pulled off the narrow country lane and rode into the thick trees, finding a safe place to conceal his bike. Using long, bushy branches pulled from nearby trees, he covered it over. Then he walked through the forest to find Julios waiting in the van.

Darkness fell fast. As the two men waited, Harvey's pulse raised and fell with each sporadic passing car.

"John was asking about you," Julios said eventually. "I spoke to him this morning while you ran."

"What was he asking?"

"He's just concerned. You keep asking him about your parents."

"He knows something."

"That's not my concern."

"Tell me, Julios. Were you around when they found us?"

"I was. You know I was."

"Where did they find us?"

"What did John tell you?"

"That's not what I asked."

"What did he tell you?"

"In his bar, after closing. We were in a booth. I was in a hamper and Hannah sat beside me."

"Then you know. Stop chasing nothing. It's clouding your judgment."

"It's not the full story," said Harvey.

"I know nothing more," said Julios, attempting to end the conversation.

But Harvey had caught the thread between his teeth.

"You too? I thought I could at least count on you."

"You can count on me, as you have always done, to keep you alive," Julios snapped.

"You know something?"

"All I know is that if you do not get your head out of ancient history and into the game, we will both be killed. Snap out of it," Julios ordered.

Then he slid out of the van just as a black Range Rover nosed into the small space.

"Recognise him?" asked Julios, as Harvey climbed outside.

"The windows are tinted. I can't see his face," replied Harvey, joining Julios in front of the van.

The Range Rover parked in front of the entrance, leaving enough room for another van to enter and park.

"Do you think that's them?" asked Harvey.

"Why would they park over there?" said Julios. "No. It's a babysitter. He's there to make sure we don't try to rip them off."

Harvey checked his watch.

"Any minute now."

CHAPTER TWENTY-EIGHT

"I knew it," said Harvey. "They're up to something."

Julios looked at Harvey, whose eyes tracked the driver as he turned the van and reversed up alongside theirs.

"That's my *target*," said Harvey.

"Your target?" asked Julios.

"Shaun Tyson."

"Him?" said Julios. "He's a-"

"He's out on bail. Preys on little girls."

"We're here for the guns, Harvey. Keep your little hobby out of this," said Julios.

"But why is he working for Thomson?"

"I said keep your hobby out of this. Stay professional. Stay alert."

But deep inside Harvey's stomach, the beast had awoken at the sight of Shaun Tyson. A long finger reached up and clawed at Harvey's chest. The beast was hungry.

"*Harvey,*" snapped Julios, bringing Harvey back from his stare. "I'll watch the Range Rover. You check the guns."

The driver's door opened and Shaun Tyson stepped down to the ground. He glanced back at the Range Rover then returned his nervous eyes to flick between Harvey and Julios.

"Friend of yours?" asked Harvey.

Shaun nodded. He seemed reluctant to step past Harvey to open the back of the van.

"Open the doors," said Harvey. "And don't try anything stupid."

A growl from Harvey's stomach sent a wave of energy through his body as Shaun stepped past him. His eyes pulsed as a dose of adrenaline released into his bloodstream. Harvey pulled his handgun from the waistband of his cargo pants and aimed at the doors, ready for someone to jump out.

But nobody did. Inside was a wooden crate on a pallet and nothing else.

Having opened the rear doors, Shaun

stepped back out of Harvey's way. They were all in full view of the mystery car. Harvey made the gun safe and tucked it away. Then he drew his knife.

The movement frightened Shaun, and he stepped back, his eyes wide with fear. Searching inside the boy's eyes, Harvey found nothing but the desire to tear him limb from limb. He found himself imagining how he would kill him. It would be slow and it would be painful.

Julios joined them at the back of the van and positioned himself where he could see both the boy and the Range Rover. He'd pulled his own handgun from his waist and let it hang at his side in clear view. A warning to whoever was in the car.

"Are you going to stand there looking at the boy? Or are you going to get the guns?" said Julios, once more snapping Harvey from his thoughts.

Removing the wooden lid of the crate required little effort. Using his knife to pry it from the box, Harvey let it fall to the van's floor with a deafening boom like a bass drum. Inside, as expected, were twelve Heckler and Koch MP-5s.

Harvey reached in to check the serial numbers had been removed as agreed. He tested the action and slotted one of the twenty-four magazines in and out.

"They're new. They're clean," he called out to Julios.

"Okay. Move them out," said Julios.

"I need the money first," said Shaun. His voice wavered. "You can't take them until you give me the money."

Shaun's voice was weak as if he were a lamb. And Harvey felt like a wolf. He stepped down with the rifle in his hands. Ignoring Shaun's weak request, he opened the door to his own van and lay down the gun at one end of a thick blanket inside. Then Harvey returned his attention to Shaun.

"They said I had to take the money or-"

"Or what?" said Harvey. "Or your friend will take the money from me?"

"I'm not looking for trouble," said Shaun. "I was just told-"

"Just pay the boy," said Julios. A wry and very rare grin crept onto his face beneath the bored expression. "Let's get this over with."

From his jacket pocket, Harvey produced an envelope. He held it at head height, weighing it in his hand and studying Shaun's face, remembering every minute detail. He took a step towards the boy, peering into his eyes and enjoying the fear that ran across his face like a stampede of weakness.

"Now, now," Julios cautioned Harvey. "Play nicely."

Harvey slapped the envelope of money against Shaun's chest. For the briefest of moments, as Shaun reached up to take it, their hands connected. It felt as if a pulse of electricity burst into his veins. Harvey reeled.

"Are you going to help or are you going to just stand there?" asked Harvey.

Shaun returned his look but did not speak. He took a step back, pocketing the envelope. His eyes darted from the van to the Range Rover and back to Harvey.

"You get them out and pass them to me," said Harvey.

"I'm not allowed," said Shaun, his voice stuttering. "They said I wasn't-"

But Shaun's refusal was broken by Harvey snatching his gun from his waist and placing the muzzle against Shaun's temple.

"In the van, now," he said.

One by one, Shaun passed Harvey the

remaining eleven weapons, which Harvey covered with the blanket before slamming the doors to his van. Beads of nervous sweat had formed on Shaun's forehead. When he jumped down to close the doors of his own van, he seemed relieved to be out and for the episode to be over.

But as he moved to walk towards the driver's door, Harvey blocked his path. The urge to reach out and grab the boy's throat was strong. The beast inside him was ready.

"Are we done?" said Julios, breaking the tension.

Harvey stepped to one side, allowing Shaun to pass him and run to the front of the van. The engine started before the door had even closed. The wheels spun as Shaun, in his desperation to get away, fumbled with the pedals. Harvey and Julios watched the van disappear onto the lane and waited for the Range Rover to follow. But it remained stationary.

"Let's go," said Harvey, climbing into the van. "Drop me at my bike and I'll follow."

But something had caught Julios' attention. He walked to the centre of the clearing, staring into the Range Rover as if his gaze could cut through the tinted windows.

Every sense in Harvey's body came alive in an instant.

His eyes flicked from Julios to the car. The driver's window lowered.

Julios reached for his weapon.

A handgun emerged through the window.

Dropping to one knee, Julios raised his gun and aimed.

The two men opened fire.

Harvey leapt from the van, pulling his gun as the Range Rover lurched into action. Its wheels span as it sped from the scene. Harvey opened fire, shattering the car windows and bursting its tyres. The black bodywork was peppered with bullet holes. As Harvey released the magazine and slammed a fresh one into place, at the very edge of his vision, he saw Julios lying face-first on the ground.

CHAPTER TWENTY-NINE

The huge **SUV** bounced over the body of Julios Saville. All around Frank, glass shattered. A single bullet tore through the car's interior, ricocheted past Frank's ear and shattered the windscreen, leaving a sprawling web of finger-like cracks and a thumb-sized hole in the glass.

The two blown tyres hindered his turn out of the clearing. As Frank hauled on the wheel with his foot flat on the accelerator, the front end of the car tore through a hedgerow, kicking up dirt and sliding from side to side as the remaining rubber searched for grip.

Daring once to look up and check his rear-view mirror, Frank saw the dark shape of the surviving man run into the road. He raised his weapon and emptied the remainder of his magazine into the back of Frank's car. The rear window shattered. When the shooting finally stopped, Frank pulled himself up from where he was ducked below the line of fire. The two blown tyres pulled him to one side, forcing Frank to use all his strength to keep the car straight.

The end of the road was in view, but the ordeal had been too much for the car. Thick plumes of white smoke poured from the engine bay. With the windscreen shattered and full of holes, and every other window blown away, it soon began to fill the car. Hanging his head out the window, Frank managed to reach the junction where a left turn would take him onto the M11 motorway south, and a right turn would take him north. Straight on would take him into the Essex countryside.

The remainder of one of the tyres pulled free from the wheel and shot off to the left. A shower of sparks flew up into Frank's face as the wheel cut into the tarmac road. Seeing no other choice, he forced the car forward, knowing the man would be right behind.

The motorway passed below him and the

darkness of the countryside closed in on all sides. But with no lights to see by and his eyes sore from the smoking engine, only glimpses of the tree line to the side of the road guided Frank onward.

Until the dark line of trees disappeared.

And the angry rumble of the wheels on the road stopped.

For the second time in two days, Frank's broken body was tossed around inside a rolling car. His head smashed into the door frame then the steering wheel. Broken glass rained down on him, and huge scoops of dirt ripped from the ground and flew into his face. The car came to a stop on its roof at the foot of a steep embankment in a wash of angry steam and smoke.

His body screamed at him, unable to tell old bruises from new. Frank gracelessly lowered himself to the roof amongst the shards of glass and dirt. A loud whining rang in his ear as if he'd just stepped from a loud nightclub, and a trickle of blood ran into his eye from a vague cut somewhere on his head.

Close by, an engine approached. The sound of tyres on gravel. A flicker of headlights.

Then nothing.

The desire to give up was overwhelming, but something inside Frank, something stronger than he knew, pushed him on. He reached for his gun, which lay among the broken glass and dirt.

A van door slammed. Frank recognised the sound.

With slow and tender movements, Frank eased himself into the prone position, aiming at the embankment through the rear window as footsteps made their way through the long grass.

In the darkness beyond the car, two legs appeared. They stopped, as if the owner was searching the scene, then eased forward.

In his mind, among wild thoughts of the killer's eyes and of the death he faced, Frank tried to recall how many shots he had already fired.

But the footsteps came closer. Just two legs.

The pulse of his heartbeat was deafening. The throb of his bruised legs and ribs was excruciating. The blood that flowed from a wound on his torn skin blinded him in one eye. His gun shook in his hands. His finger curled around the trigger, ready to squeeze, and at last, when the dark outline of a head peered into view through the empty window, Frank pulled the trigger.

But the hammer fell on an empty chamber.

CHAPTER THIRTY

The motionless form of Harvey's mentor, best friend and only companion lay still, face down in the mud. In his hand, the gun he'd cleaned with meticulous regularity was filled with the same dirt that stained the man's face. His fat finger still rested on the trigger and his strong hand still clutched the grip.

A single tyre mark ran across the width of his body and a hole in his neck identified the kill shot. Blood no longer oozed from the wound, but Julios' face and overcoat still wore the evidential spatter. It was inky black in the dark night.

Dropping to his knees alongside his friend and with his own gun in his hand, Harvey took in the sight as if he'd borne the brunt of the gunfire himself. A stab of pain in his chest tightened and a rhythmic pounding of anguish in his head created the urge to scream out loud into the silent sky above.

A familiar scratching of a long, hungry finger teased Harvey's mind with thoughts of retribution. It filled him with images of pain and suffering. Harvey knelt, indulging in the promise of revenge until, at last, he said goodbye to his friend.

"I'll come back for you."

Harvey cast a fleeting glimpse at the van and made his way toward his bike, fuelled by a deep craving. It was a craving he'd felt only once before as a child standing behind a man in the darkness.

Colliding with trees invisible among the shadows, Harvey made his way through the thick forest. Blinded by his desire to find the man in the Range Rover, Harvey stumbled into his bike. Drunk with passion, loss and fatigue, he manoeuvred onto the narrow country lane. The relentless beast inside him was scratching its way out, controlling his thoughts and guiding every action.

The rear wheel spun with a snatch of his

wrist and release of the clutch. Harvey felt the beating heart of the bike as if it were a part of him. He worked through the gears, winding the engine up to full speed. Every sensory organ in his body was alive to his surroundings. The world shot past in a blur of dark shapes and darker shadows until light crept in and the winding snake-like motorway lay before him. It enticed his poisoned mind with an open space in which to ride and scream and shout at the top of his lungs. So fast that nobody could hear. So carefree that cars he passed were merely indistinct stationary objects.

The hot metal of the bike warmed the insides of Harvey's legs in stark contrast to the bite of the cold air on his numbed fingers and face.

And without warning, the world appeared real once more.

He slowed to a crawl and moved across to the slow lane, allowing cars he had passed moments before in a heightened state of delirious mourning to speed by as if the world hadn't noticed the death of Julios Saville.

Coming to a stop on the shoulder, he switched off the engine and warmed his hands on the fuel tank. To his left, rolling fields and trees seamlessly met the dark horizon, masking where one ended and the other began. But somewhere in that layer of dark unknown, there was unfathomable beauty, a dawning of realisation. It struck Harvey as hard as the deaths of his best friend, Julios, and the only person he'd ever loved, Hannah.

A calm wash of cool blood filled his veins, easing the craving inside him and stroking the wild emotions that had run riot. It was then that he knew. In that moment. When a world of fields and trees and the massive expanse of sky joined hands hidden by shadows, the answer came to him.

CHAPTER THIRTY-ONE

"Sir? Are you in there? Are you okay?" asked Melody.

Her voice struck a chord in Frank, forcing him to exhale with audible relief.

"Sir, can you hear me? We're going to get you out."

Every muscle in Frank's body relaxed. His head dropped to the glass-riddled roof of the car. He let go of the weapon. His eyes, after all the fear, tension and adrenaline, released a single tear. Muffled voices approached and flashlights switched on to show the full extent of the damage. Shielding his eyes from the bright light, Frank reached forward to grasp the hand of Denver Cox.

"How did you know where to find me?" said Frank, ashamed to hear the tremble in his voice.

"Tenant tracked your phone, sir," said Melody. "We found a strange message from an unknown number when we restored your mobile."

"The location?"

"Yes, sir. So when we couldn't find you at the hospital, we figured this is where you'd be. I'm sorry if we overstepped the mark, sir. We were worried."

"Possibly the best police work you've done this week, Mills," said Frank with a laugh that sent a wave of sharp pain through his ribs. He grimaced, sucking in air through his teeth to control the agony.

"Let's get you to the hospital, sir," said Melody.

"No," said Frank. "We need to go back."

"To where, sir? We saw the van leave. And the motorbike, too."

"You'll see," said Frank.

With the help of Cox, step by step, he walked up the embankment to the team's old VW Transporter van. Frank was helped into the passenger side, Cox drove, and Mills and

Tenant sat in the back. A workbench had been built along one side, where Tenant had fixed two computer screens. Below the bench was a computer and a network of cables splayed out in all directions, including along the chassis of the vehicle to the roof, where the VSAT antenna was fixed for mobile internet access. In a space behind the front seats, Melody stored her surveillance equipment and sniper rifle.

They drove back over the motorway and toward the scene of the crime where, less than thirty minutes previously, Frank had engaged in a shootout. The memory seemed a lifetime ago.

"Is this the right road?" said Frank. "I don't remember that bend and I don't remember that field."

"Shock, sir," said Melody from behind, as Cox turned the little van into the clearing and stopped at the entrance. "You'll be amazed at the things it can do to your mind."

In front of them, lit by the headlights and alien to its surroundings, was the body of Julios Saville.

The team were silent for a few seconds as they took in the sight. The van parked to the right had three bullet holes in the bonnet, which must have been from Frank, although he had no recollection of shooting them.

"Did you manage to find my camera?" Frank asked nobody in particular.

"We did, sir," said Tenant. "It was water damaged, but I recovered the files. The camera is a write-off, I'm afraid."

"Forget about the camera. Did you run the facial recognition?"

The team were silent once again.

"Sir?" began Melody. "What exactly happened here? That's Julios Saville. He's been wanted for more than twenty years. The rider, we strongly believe, is the vigilante that we've been hunting for over a decade. What's the connection?"

"Cox, Tenant, load Mr Saville into the back, would you?"

The two operatives acknowledged the order and got to work.

"Mills, help me out."

Every movement seemed to find a new nerve ending with a new feeling of pain. But with slow steps and the help of Melody, Frank walked to the back of the white van. Then he paused. Before he opened the door, he turned to face Melody.

"Mills, you're my number one," he began. "You're a credit to the force and I honestly don't know what I'd do without you. Without any of you. You, Cox and Tenant, you're what we used to call a dream team."

"Thank you, sir," replied Mills. She was maintaining her professionalism but unable to hide the perplexed expression in her furrowed brow.

"You've got a great career ahead of you. You all have. But while you might be the smartest person I ever met, sometimes, Mills, you need to trust your instinct. Even if your instinct seems to be leading you against the grain." He lowered his voice. "And sometimes you have to do things that are...questionable."

"Sir?" said Mills.

She was desperate to see inside the van to see what Frank was hiding.

"That man over there is a promotion, Mills. No question. He's been wanted for two decades, and although we have no proof, we know he's responsible for more murders than you can imagine."

"I saw on his file, sir. He's a catch, alright."

"And inside here," continued Frank, "is a god damn medal."

He pulled open the doors, tossed the blanket to one side, and stepped back to let Mills take in the view of twelve Heckler and Koch MP-5s, dark and heavy, but glistening in the moonlight.

CHAPTER THIRTY-TWO

"It's over. I'm out," said Harvey, slamming the door to John's home office.

The entrance was far removed from Harvey's usual silent approach, and John stood in surprise for a second before a lifetime of wealth and power helped him regain control.

"What do you mean you're out?" replied John, sinking back down. "What's happened?"

"It's all lies. There's no truth to any of it, is there?" said Harvey.

"What do you mean, Son?" said John. "And remember who you're talking to."

"I know who I'm talking to, John. I'm done with it. I'm done with the lies."

"I don't understand."

"The hamper, the pub, the blankets, and the made-up story about how you found us. It's all lies."

"Harvey," said John, "take it easy. What's brought this on?"

"I suppose you know about Hannah too, don't you?"

"Hannah?" said John, surprised to hear Harvey mention her name.

"You know what happened to her, don't you?" said Harvey. "That night. The night she cut herself to ribbons in shame."

"No, Harvey, I-"

"Well, I know. It was Jack. And if I knew, then you damn well knew too. And he wasn't alone, was he?"

"Listen, Son. I don't know what's happened. But you need to calm yourself down. Here, have a drink," said John, passing Harvey his crystal tumbler of brandy with the remains of three ice cubes floating on the surface.

Harvey took the drink then launched it across the room. Glass shattered to the hardwood floor and a golden stain edged its way across the flock wallpaper.

"You need to start telling some truths, John. You see all this?" Harvey swept his hand through the air. "I'll burn it to the ground and I'll take you with it."

With practised composure, John straightened the cuffs of his shirt, a habit he'd formed and a sign he was processing information. Walking from behind his desk, following a well-trodden path to his drinks cabinet, he poured himself a fresh brandy. Three chinks of ice against crystal preceded a gurgling decanter, which was then placed in its spot on the silver tray. With his back to Harvey, John sipped at his drink. He puckered his lips then returned to his place behind the desk and rested his forearms on the black leather inlay.

"Where's Julios?" he asked, his voice calm and controlled.

"Facedown in the mud with a bullet hole in his neck," replied Harvey.

John sipped at his drink, not the faintest of emotions betraying his thoughts.

"That's why you're upset," said John. "It's natural."

A pulse of life bulged at Harvey's eyes.

"What about the guns?" continued John.

But it was too late.

In one smooth move, Harvey had reached over, grabbed his foster father by his neck and dragged him across the desk to the parquet floor, gripping his throat with one strong hand.

"Give me one good reason why I shouldn't kill you right now," said Harvey, his voice hoarse with tension as he squeezed the life from John Cartwright.

But John stared back with a reproachful eye. Any sign of his struggle was masked by years of control, lies and deceit.

"I know who killed Hannah," he rasped.

A stab of the beast's sharp claws. Harvey released his grip.

"You want to know?"

John slapped Harvey's hand away and pushed himself to his feet. He smoothed his trousers, flattened his hair and straightened his cuffs then moved back to his place behind the desk where, once more, he took his seat.

"Sit down," said John.

Harvey didn't react.

"I said sit down," said John, louder and more forceful.

The two men locked eyes, daring each other to break, testing the other man's resolve.

"Have it your way," said John, sipping at his drink. "But be warned, what I tell you will destroy you."

"No, John," replied Harvey. "*You* destroyed me with your lies. You destroyed me when you had Julios train me. You bred me to be a killer because your own son was too spineless."

"You won't antagonise me, Harvey. I love you both. But as much as I love you both, you're both flawed."

Harvey didn't reply.

"I'll do a deal. It's a one-time offer."

"I know your deals well enough."

"It's a one-time offer," continued John, ignoring Harvey's comment. "You do one last job for me-"

"I told you. It's over," said Harvey. He pushed off the desk and paced the room, turning back to John only when the rage inside him showed a momentary lapse. "There will be no more jobs."

"You'll do one more job for me, Harvey Stone if it's the last thing you do," said John. His voice had raised well beyond its normal volume and the fire in his wide eyes was burning with anger.

"And what?" said Harvey. "I do one last job for you, so you can screw me over one last time. Is that it?"

"You do one last job for your old man," replied John, his voice lower, calmer and the tone softer. "For me. Like the old days."

Harvey met his foster father's eyes with a raised eyebrow, waiting for the finish.

"And I'll tell you who raped Hannah."

CHAPTER THIRTY-THREE

"Capone, *how you doing?*" asked Rob in a mock Italian accent as Shaun approached.

He and Lenny were unloading boxes and sacks from the van.

"I'm okay. Terry said to come and help you. He said he needs some time alone. What can I do?"

"Listen, Shaun. You're not really a people person, are you?"

"Eh?"

"You may have been *told* to come and help, but you don't need to tell us you've been told to come and help. Right, Rob?"

"That's right, Lenny."

Shaun looked confused.

"See, if you had walked up to us and said, 'Hey guys, can I help you?' we would've just thought it was your exceedingly good nature that brought you out into the cold, and we'd have appreciated the gesture. But being told to come out here means that you are, in fact, reluctant to help but will do it because the boss said so. Right?"

"I guess," replied Shaun, unsure if he should be helping or not.

"He *guesses*, Rob."

Lenny climbed into the rear of the van and pulled a few boxes to the edge before jumping down. Rob snorted at Shaun and then carried on shifting the boxes to a neat pile in the corner.

"What are you doing, anyway?"

"We're emptying the van, Shaun. What does it look like we're doing?" said Lenny, as he dropped another box carefully to the ground.

"What is all this stuff?

"It's all the food for Bradley's wake," said Lenny. "Blimey, he doesn't stop asking questions. Does he, Rob?"

"No, mate, he doesn't stop asking questions."

"You know what, Rob?"

"What's that, Lenny?"

"I seem to *remember* something about questions," said Lenny. "It was something the boss said about asking too many of them."

Shaun looked at the floor. He'd thought he'd won some respect from the two men, but they were both still as mean as ever.

"Oh, *I* remember that," said Rob. He stopped and leaned on a large wooden crate. "What *was* it now? Was it, if you ask too many questions, you get to lay in a big cosy bed all day, and the boss would pay for hookers to come and keep you company?"

"No, I don't think so, Rob. That doesn't ring any bells. Was it, if you ask too many questions, the boss will make you a roast dinner with all the trimmings and serve it to you while you watch the football?"

"Hmmm, no, I don't think it was that either," said Rob. He laughed as he took two sacks from Lenny. "I'm sure it had *something* to do with..."

"*Pigs*," they both said at the same time.

"That's it," said Lenny. "Pigs."

"If you ask too many questions, the boss will feed you to the pigs."

"Alright, alright. I get it," said Shaun, and turned away.

The two men laughed at his dejection and removed the last of the boxes from the van.

"Look, Shaun, if you really want to help, grab that sack over there and the roll of gaffer tape," said Lenny.

Shaun looked around and found an old hessian sack on the floor and the gaffer tape on a shelf above it. He passed them to Lenny who threw them into the back of the van.

"Is that it?" Shaun asked.

"Easy, eh?" said Lenny.

"One day you'll be as good as us at moving boxes and passing the gaffer tape," said Rob.

"Is that *more* guns?" said Shaun, pointing to a wooden crate.

"I don't believe it, Rob."

"I'm flabbergasted, Len."

"What?" said Shaun.

Shaun's world turned black as the sack was forced over his head and he was thrown into the back of the van.

CHAPTER THIRTY-FOUR

"I don't know how the old man does it. Imagine having your son killed and still being able to hold it together enough to plan the northern job, sell guns to Cartwright *and* arrange the funeral."

Harvey watched from the shadows to the side of the house as the larger of the two men spoke.

"Yeah, I feel for him," said the other. "I did ask if we could help, but he said he'd take care of it. He said he wanted to do it. Like it was some kind of parental obligation."

"You think he feels guilty?"

"For what? Bradley? No. Bradley walked the line, and he knew it. We all do, right?"

"Yeah, I know what you mean. Do you ever think about getting out before it's too late?"

"What do you mean too late?"

"You know, getting killed. Seems like it's getting serious again. Bradley's dead. That guy at the gun deal. I even heard the old man talking to that bloke on the phone. You know he killed Donny Cartwright?"

"What bloke?"

"You know." The man began to talk in hushed tones. "The bloke he gets to *take care of business*."

"None of it makes sense, mate. As for getting out, do you really think you could walk away from all this with your knees intact? Do you honestly reckon Terry would let you?"

"Hold on. Keep it down, Rob."

Footsteps approached across the gravel, but from where Harvey was hiding, the newcomer was out of sight. An image of the scene formed in his mind.

"Capone, *how you doing?*" said one of the men.

"I'm okay. Terry said to come and help you. He said he needs some time alone. What can I do?"

In an instant, Harvey placed the weak voice. The image in his mind evolved to include Shaun Tyson. As the conversation between the two men and Tyson played on, Harvey's imagination digressed into scenes of twisted retribution.

"Is that *more* guns?"

The question snapped Harvey from his wild daydream. A rare smile crept onto his face as a plan formulated.

"I don't believe it, Rob."

"I'm flabbergasted, Len."

"What?" asked the simple voice.

Muffled, panicked screams and anguished cries were followed by gaffer tape stripped off a roll then the thud of Tyson's body hitting the wooden floor of the van. Rear doors slammed with thundering booms in the night. The scene played out with brutal attention to detail in Harvey's head.

"*Questions*, Shaun. We told you," said one of the men, and banged on the side of the van.

"Do you want to take him now or in the morning?" asked one man to the other.

"I'm bleeding knackered, Rob. But tomorrow's Bradley's funeral. It's going to be hell."

The van fired into life, coughing black

diesel smoke from its exhaust, and the driver found first gear with a crunch of the gearbox.

Harvey made his move.

Making almost no sound, he slipped behind the vehicle, placed one foot on the rear bumper and found two handholds. The moment the van lurched into action, Harvey put his full weight onto the bumper, timing the shift with the rising of the clutch and movement of the vehicle.

Clinging to the rear doors, his view was restricted. His plan was vague but options had been limited. The driver turned right out of the courtyard, steering the van along the empty country lane where overgrown trees scraped the sides and scratched his face. The driver stopped only once, at a T-junction at the end of the lane. The break gave Harvey precious moments to adjust his fingers and search for a better handhold.

But the journey was short. They had travelled less than a mile by Harvey's estimates when the van slowed and pulled into a working farm. It continued down a bumpy track between huge barns and machinery sheds.

The main house, which was set back from

the rest of the buildings, appeared old, dark, and poorly maintained, while the barns seemed to be well kept. Fresh mud flicked from the wheels as the van passed through a field, sliding and fighting for grip. The driver stayed in first gear, keeping the revs low. It was as if he knew the track well, seeking the higher dry patches of ground amid the thick glutinous mud.

Their arrival created a disturbance in the livestock. Headlights shone two bright beams of light onto the end of the track. The vehicle shuddered to a stop. Dropping to the ground, Harvey crawled beneath the van just as the two front doors opened.

"Time to meet your maker, Shauny," said the driver, banging the side of the van

Harvey heard muffled whines and screams followed by scuffled struggles on the van's wooden floor as the rear doors opened and the two men pulled out Tyson and dropped him into the mud. His hands were bound behind his back and his heavy breathing was loud through the sack over his head.

Both men delivered a few taunting kicks to their prisoner, seeming to enjoy the warm-up to the main event. The hessian sack was ripped off Tyson's head, but the kicks had left him breathless and he lay face down in the mud, his eyes shining with the guilty tears of a condemned man. A strip of gaffer tape had been placed across his mouth and the muffled screaming began. It was high like the cries of a child.

"Right," said one of the men. "Let's get him up and into the pen so we can get out of here."

"Here, Lenny. How about a little wager?"

"What? Like last time?" replied Lenny.

"Yeah. How long do you reckon he'll last?"

The man called Lenny seemed to consider his answer, giving Shaun time to look around, hopeful for the smallest chance of survival. His eyes fell on Harvey, who raised his index finger to his lips in the international sign for silence.

"I reckon less than a minute," said the first man. "He's not exactly a fighter, is he?"

"Alright, you're on. Ten quid?"

"Done," said the man.

Behind them, a chorus of grunting pigs chimed in.

"Don't worry, Shauny. The noise excites the pigs. They love it. Gets them all horny or hungry. One of the two. I doubt young Shaun would mind if they get a bit frisky, would you? Dirty little perv would probably enjoy it."

With wide, pleading eyes, Shaun held Harvey's stare for a second longer before he disappeared from view, dragged out of sight by the two men.

Harvey set to work.

Sliding in the mud beneath the van, he turned to watch as the men dragged Tyson towards a huge pig pen a few metres away. With slow, deliberate movements, Harvey rolled from his hiding place and walked into the open until he was standing just five feet behind them.

"Here piggy," called one of the men.

"What are you doing?" asked the other.

"I'm calling the pigs over."

"Pigs don't respond to being called. They respond to being fed."

Shaun struggled harder. His muffled screams grew higher and louder. As if sensing the weakness in the air, one by one, the pigs came to the fence, fighting for the prime posi-tion. Their size was impressive. They were the biggest swine Harvey had ever seen, fat, bulky shadows wallowing in the dark mud. But it was the noise they made that impressed him the most. The loud grunts and snorts of the hogs gave no indication of their number, but the sound was chaotic. Harvey used it to mask the sound of his own attack.

Switching his gun to his left hand, Harvey drew his knife with his right. Then he stepped behind the larger of the two men, who were both leaning on the fence, antagonising the hogs with imitations of farm animals.

In one swift movement, Harvey reached around and sliced the big man's throat. Raising his gun hand, he aimed at the man's friend. Harvey forced the dying man up onto the fence until his weight carried him over. He fell to the ground inside the pen with a slap, trying in vain to hold the two flaps of his neck together and stem the flow of blood.

All the pigs silenced, stopped and stared at the twitching body.

As the alpha made his way through the mud, driven on by the irony scent of blood, the second man, in horror, slowly turned to face Harvey, who stood grim-faced with his weapon aimed at the man's chest.

In disbelief, the man's gaze flicked from his dying friend to Harvey and back again.

No words were spoken. Both men weighed their odds. The largest of the hogs took its first tentative bite of the dead man's flesh.

"Do you know what you've just done?" the surviving man said to Harvey, shaking his head, still dumbstruck by the turn of events.

"Put your hands on the fence where I can see them."

"Do you even know who we are?"

A wild and furious bout of grunting announced the hog's approval of the man's flesh and the whole pack descended on the body.

"I don't care who you are. Put your hands on the fence," replied Harvey, shouting to be heard above the grunts and crunching of bones.

"What are you going to do? Shoot me?"

The man placed both hands on the fence. The alpha hog caught the movement. He carried on with his meal but kept a watchful eye on the second course.

A single gunshot found the mud behind the man's boot.

"The fence," said Harvey. "Climb it."

"What? No."

Harvey didn't reply. He just locked eyes with the man, reading his next moves and drinking in his fear.

"No. No, you're going to have to shoot me."

The man searched the darkness around him for help.

"We're alone. And you can run but you won't get far," said Harvey.

Then he paused, allowing the man time to consider his options.

"What's your name?" asked Harvey.

"Rob," the man replied after considering a lie.

"Okay, Rob," said Harvey. "Do you think you can make it to the other side of the pen before the pigs get you?"

"Are you *crazy*? What? No."

"How about a wager? You do gamble, don't you?"

Wide eyes glistening with fear stared back at Harvey as he stepped closer.

"If you can make it to the other side, I'll let you live."

The man silently considered the distance.

"Keep your hands on the fence," said Harvey

Harvey glanced across at the remains of the man in the pen.

"Now is your chance," said Harvey. "I'd go while they're busy eating your friend. But there doesn't seem to be much of him left."

A hog grunted behind Harvey as if confirming the fact.

The rise and falls of Rob's chest were clearly visible. He psyched himself up with three loud exhales, his hands gripping the top bar of the fence like it was his only lifeline. Then, as the first of the pigs looked up from its meal, sniffing the air for fresh blood, Rob lunged upwards. He vaulted the fence, landing on both feet in the mud with a loud slap.

Before he could make a move, before his feet had stopped sliding, and before he'd let go of the fence, Harvey swung his arm in a wide arc and jammed the point of his knife through Rob's hand. It stabbed deeply into the soft wooden post, pinning Rob to the spot. His eyes flicked from his hand to Harvey and then to the pigs, who had reduced the dead man to nothing but a few gnawed bones in the mud.

"No. No. No," Rob said, his voice high like a child's.

"You lose," said Harvey.

"Let me go. No. Stop. Don't leave me here."

He gave constant nervous glances back at the increasingly interested hogs.

The biggest of the animals took a step towards him, sniffing the air for fear.

In desperation, Rob seized the knife with his free hand and tried to pull it from the wood, turning it left and right, his face contorting with every tiny movement of the blade. But the knife held fast. With a final effort, his bloodied hand slipped from the handle. The hogs took another step closer.

"Help me, you bastard," Rob breathed, his throat closed with fear and panic.

Harvey didn't reply.

A hog stepped closer, sniffing at the man's leg.

"Get off me," screamed Rob, kicking out at the animal, which only angered the beast and intrigued its appetite.

Seeing no alternative as the hogs closed in, Rob caught Harvey's stare, reminding him in that instant of the lengths a man will go to live. With his teeth bared and as the first of the hogs sank its jaw into the back of his leg, Rob pulled his hand from the blade.

He roared as if he'd become a beast himself as his hand split around the sharp blade until just a small slice of flesh and sinew held fast to the fence. He tugged his hand free with a whimper.

But it was too late.

The weight of the hogs bore down on Rob, and their razor-sharp teeth clamped onto any piece of his body they could find.

Harvey turned away, picked up Shaun's leg and dragged his own quarry to the van.

CHAPTER THIRTY-FIVE

No lights lit the courtyard of the farmhouse at the foot of the hill, but Frank knew it was the right place even in the darkness. He eased the door of the rental car closed, leaving it unlocked to avoid the brief flashing of lights. As if he were out for a late evening stroll in the countryside, he ambled along the lane towards freedom or death.

But the charade of a night time stroller was unnecessary. Not a single car passed or even drove near to the road. Frank had time to breathe the air, smell the fields, and admire the wide-open expanse of nothing.

The darkness proved useful for his unobserved movements around the side of the three buildings and into the rear garden. Peaks of tall conifers reached high into the sky. The light from a single ground-floor window illuminated the grass and gravel garden.

Inside the house, a familiar shape passed by the window. The man leaned against a grand, brick-built fireplace with a solid oak mantle, which sat beneath a mirror framed with ornate mouldings of silver and bronze.

Terry Thomson stared at his reflection with a seething look of contempt. It was the stare of a guilty man who had, at last, discovered a conscience amongst the rotting lies that blackened his heart.

Looking on with voyeuristic pleasure, Frank felt a connection to the broken man. Terry had held his career on a knife-edge. He'd used blackmail to coerce Frank into diverting police resources, which had resulted in lie upon lie to compound, blocking promotions and opportunities while those around Frank had soared.

But the end was in sight and the path of freedom grew close.

Fingering the trigger of his weapon, Frank savoured each passing moment the way a hunter might relish his prey moments before taking a life. Foreplay before the act of death.

A rush of pleasure ran through his body, unlike anything he had felt for years.

A sigh fell from his throat, involuntary and loud in the silence.

And a tingle twitched his fingers.

Terry, wearing a gown of deep red silk fastened with a similar belt, sank the amber contents of his glass in a single mouthful. The burn in his throat was masked by his already reddened eyes. A bottle of brandy stood nearby on a wooden drinks cabinet. The lid was off. Terry's current drink was neither his first nor last.

Enjoying the power, Frank allowed Terry Thomson one last drink, and Terry poured a careless measure. Beside the bottle was an old record player, finished with synthetic wooden veneer and adorned with chromed dials and trim. It was much like the one Frank had owned in the seventies, which had fed him delights such as Led Zeppelin and Pink Floyd. But from the shadows, the label on the LP Terry was playing was just a blur.

Only a few whispered teases of sound reached Frank's ears before Terry turned the volume dial. Then he stood at the mirror with his drink in hand and the wonders of Mozart building behind him with winding woodwind arpeggios. Two heavy, sustained orchestral chords struck loudly through the glass. The space between the notes seemed to fill the void between Terry and Frank. It was the opening of Mozart's Don Giovanni opera. The piece was a favourite of Frank's.

It was meant to end this way.

All those years of lies, deaths and resentment, it was all leading up to this moment. The underdog would be the last man to stand.

A framed picture of Bradley Thomson stood on the mantelpiece. It was the focus of Terry's attention. The look in Terry's eyes evoked a peculiar disposition in Frank, who was a voyeur to his enemy's suffering.

Terry raised his glass to his dead son as he stood alone. Meanwhile, Mozart faded into the soft tones that marked the halfway point of the overture. Wind instruments replaced heavy strings, and delicate tones clung to the ceiling and the walls. Then, slowly and softly, the string section increased in depth, building with each bar. Frank was transfixed. It was a solo performance, a monologue of death taking place before his eyes. The music sang the unspoken words of Thomson's expression with eerie synchronicity. The pace of the orchestra increased with the intensity of Terry's suffering.

Frank thought of the times he too had broken and worn the very same look. Times when he was alone. Times when the smallest detail reminded him of his wife. The time soon after her funeral when he'd walked mud into the house. He'd cleaned the mess before she had a chance to find it, knowing full well that she never would. He'd wished she could find it. Frank had knelt on the floor picking up pieces of loose mud, using a damp sponge to clean the rug her mother had bought them. He'd broken then, and countless other times in countless other places. At the foot of the stairs, he'd curled into a ball and sobbed like a baby. He'd cried to the point where he found his own weapon in his own hand against his own head with no recollection of the events.

The connection Frank felt for Terry grew in bitter strength as he looked on at his enemy's mourning and felt his pain and loss. He saw himself standing before the mirror, and the feeling cast a shadow over his plan. As

Frank raised the gun, eyeing the man he'd hated for so many years, a drop of cloudy doubt fogged his sight. To pull the trigger no longer carried the same weight.

His hands began to shake. His eyes lost focus. His desire to kill the man was countered by knowing the bullet would be easing his pain and suffering. Terry deserved to suffer. The two emotions gripped Frank's finger in an emotional tug of war. He could bear it no longer and his hands shook with the tension. Lowering his weapon and wiping the tears from his eyes, Frank stared through the glass at his final failed mission.

The gun fell from Frank's hand and clattered to the ground.

He watched Terry turn his back to the fire and face the doorway. His lips moved, silent to Frank but audible to the shadow that passed before the window. A shadow with a knife in its hand.

No fear seemed to engulf Terry as the intruder stepped closer. Instead, a look of defiance shone from his dark eyes and taut mouth, betrayed only by a single tear. Then, as if welcoming death, Terry opened his arms wide, raised his face to the heavens and closed his eyes.

Moving with the confidence of a man who lived for death, the shadow stepped into full view. He placed the tip of his blade onto Terry's heart but paused as if offering the man a final word.

Mozart spilt through the glass. Lips moved like a silent movie.

And steel cut flesh.

But as the first trickle of blood-stained Terry Thomson's robe and the crescendo of Mozart's masterpiece faded into the songs of whimsical flutes, Terry bore down on the hands that teased him with death. Gripping them inside his own, he forced the blade through his heart. Terry took the life from his body as if it was his final wish to die by his own hand.

Eyes opened wide and gritted teeth flashed white as Terry Thomson placed one foot into the next world. Somewhere deep inside Frank's heart, a part of him died. But in his mind, a cloud of fog lifted as the body of Terry Thomson crumpled to the floor.

And Frank took one step onto the path of freedom.

CHAPTER THIRTY-SIX

A small suitcase stood by the door to John's home office and the smell of coffee filled the air.

"It's done," said Harvey from the doorway.

"I can see, Harvey. It says so right here on the front bleeding page. The papers don't mess about, do they? Probably couldn't wait to tell the world that Terry Thomson, gangland crime lord, was killed," said John, as he looked away out of the window. "All these years we've been enemies, Harvey. You know, I think I'll miss him."

Harvey didn't reply. He allowed his foster father a moment of reflection.

"He burnt down my first bar, you know?"

"The one with the booth? Where you found a child? And a baby in a hamper wrapped in blankets?"

John glanced back but couldn't meet Harvey's eye.

"No." A hint of anger faded on John's face as quickly as it had appeared. "A different bar. Terry Thomson reckoned I was on his patch. I wasn't. On his patch, you know?"

Harvey didn't reply.

"Funny, isn't it?" said John.

"What's *funny*?"

"Life, Harvey. *Life.*"

"It depends on your sense of humour, John."

"Come to think of it, I can't remember the last time I saw you laugh, Harvey. Not properly."

"I don't remember complaining about it."

"No, of course not. You never complained about anything, really. When you were a little boy, you laughed at *everything*. Always smiling, you were."

John turned to meet Harvey's cold stare.

"Did I do okay, Son?"

"When?" asked Harvey.

"You know, as a dad. Was I a good dad?"

"As I said, I don't remember complaining."

"You had everything you needed. Right?" asked John.

"For a while."

Sensing the reference to Hannah, John pushed the conversation on as he always did.

"I'm going to miss you, Harvey. Honestly, Son. I love Donny, of course. I love you both. But there's something about you. You've got this something inside you. A way about you that any dad would be proud of. You're a special guy, Son. Don't ever let anyone tell you otherwise."

Harvey didn't respond.

"When are you leaving?" asked John.

"Depends."

"France?"

"I've found a farmhouse."

"After all this time looking? I'd say it was meant to be. Wouldn't you?"

"If you believe in all that, maybe," said Harvey.

"What are you going to do when I give you the name?"

"Do you really want to know?"

The question hung in the air like the smell of brandy in the old house.

"No. No. It's probably best I don't know," said John, straightening his cuffs and forcing a posture of strength, despite the news he was about to deliver.

Another silence fell.

"The guns?" John asked, his eyebrow raised.

"Twelve of them. In a van in the garage. You'll need to get rid of it."

"Good. Good work. Are you sure I can't convince you to stay, Harvey?"

"No. It's time."

"Okay. Okay. So you want the name then, I imagine?" said John.

He stood and walked to his liquor cupboard. It was early, but the day was already full of loss. John poured himself a finger of brandy over three ice cubes then set it down on the desk before stepping up to Harvey.

"Give your old man a hug, Son. Before I go," said John.

His arms opened as Terry Thomson's had the night before. The smell of alcohol was strong on his breath, as was the smell of Terry Thomson's. Relenting to the whims of the man who raised him, Harvey gave John a hug, breathing in the odour of coffee and brandy one last time.

They broke off. But as he walked back to his chair, John stumbled and caught the edge of the desk before finding his seat. Then he sipped at his brandy, puckered his lips, and linked his fingers as he so often did.

Harvey didn't move a muscle.

"You know who it is already, don't you?" said John.

"I have an idea," replied Harvey. "But I want to hear the words from your mouth."

"Who do you think it is?"

"This isn't a game."

"No, Harvey. It is not a game," said John, his voice rising with emotion. "It is the wish of a father saying goodbye to his son for the very last time and clinging to every word he says so he can remember the boy's voice in his old age."

"Sergio."

It was as if saying the name out loud carved the letters in stone. A verbal epitaph.

"How come you never acted on it then?" asked John. "If you knew."

"Nobody ever confirmed it. You always protected him."

"I'm sorry, Son," said John, nodding as if arguing the fact was futile.

John sat back in his chair and sipped at his brandy. He looked at Harvey no longer through the eyes of his boss, or the man who controlled his destiny, but as a father should, with kindness in his eyes.

"Sergio has served his purpose," said John. "And I suppose, to some degree, I've served mine to him."

"Where is he now?"

"I don't know," said John. "At the office probably."

"Message him. Tell him to come here. Then leave."

"Is that what you want?" asked John.

Harvey didn't reply.

"When are you leaving, Son?"

John hit send on his phone, placed it on the desk and sat back.

"I'll be gone by the time you get back," said Harvey.

For the first time, he looked away at the sight of John's moistening eyes.

For the last time, John Cartwright stood in

front of his foster son, admiring the strength in the boy he'd raised. He reached up, and with a gentle touch that had eluded Harvey all those years, John touched his cheek.

"Bye, Son."

CHAPTER THIRTY-SEVEN

A sleek Mercedes entered the grounds of John's house, but Sergio didn't drive slowly, as a man who knew he travelled towards death might.

From John's chair at his desk, Harvey watched with curiosity as the lean man climbed from his car, collected his laptop bag then hurried into the building. Demonstrating haste supported the facade Sergio had developed over the years. Ever the keen, hard-working and reliable employee.

"Harvey," said Sergio in surprise, as he entered the office.

He stopped in his tracks and searched for John.

"Today's a special day, Sergio," said Harvey.

"Where's John?"

Sergio clung to the door frame, unsure if he should step inside or run back to his car.

"Out, I guess," said Harvey. "So it's just you and me."

"When will he be back? He asked me to come. I came all the way from the office."

"What's the matter? You seem a little jumpy, Sergio."

"I asked you a question, Harvey. When will John be back?"

"I don't think it matters when John will be back. Does it?" said Harvey, pushing himself from the chair.

Sergio flinched at the movement. Still standing in the doorway, he eyed the front door then returned his attention to Harvey, tracking every move with fearful eyes.

"Why don't we go for a little walk, Sergio? Just you and me."

"No. I need to stay in case John comes back."

"Sergio, you and I are going for a little walk."

"I want to leave. I will call John."

Harvey stopped Sergio as he turned to leave. "You can do this the easy way. Or you can do this the hard way."

"What do you want?" asked Sergio.

He stood in the hallway with his back to Harvey.

"You *know* what I want, Sergio."

"You want money? I can give you money. I have access to it all. Everything."

"Money doesn't really interest me, Sergio. It's you I want."

"How about this?" said Sergio, reaching into his bag. "I can give you this."

In the seconds it took Sergio to pull a handgun from his bag, turn, and aim, Harvey had snatched his own from his waist, aimed, and fired a single shot into the side of Sergio's knee. The man fell to the floor and a wild bullet flew into the flock wallpaper behind Harvey.

A scream, wild and shrill, echoed through the huge house, deepening into the growl of an animal, cornered and scared, then the muted whimper of a man who knew it was over.

"Stop. Stop. No," cried Sergio, holding his ruined leg in both hands.

The handgun lay useless on the floor beside him. Grabbing Sergio's foot, Harvey wrenched it sideways, feeling the satisfying crunch of gristle and shattered bone. An ear-splitting scream flew from Sergio's lips with droplets of spittle until the pain overwhelmed what strength remained and he slipped into unconsciousness.

It wasn't until Harvey had reached the kitchen, dragging Sergio behind him by the remains of his leg, and opened the small wooden door to the basement, that consciousness returned in its weakest form.

An eyelid fluttered.

Recognition fixed Harvey with a silent plea for mercy. Realisation woke Sergio fully.

Harvey placed the sole of his boot against Sergio's back then shoved him forward onto the cold, hard concrete steps. Harvey watched with intrigue as Sergio bounced from stair to stair, his damaged leg bending awkwardly off the walls. He landed in a crumpled heap on the floor below. Harvey followed, his steps slow. It was a time he had dreamed of for so many years. He would cherish the moment.

The basement ceiling was ten feet high with thick oak beams running the full length of the building supported by oak columns of even greater thickness. At the edge of the room, dust sheets covered decades of the Cartwrights' belongings, heirlooms, toys, kitchen equipment and boxes of memories that nobody wished to remember.

Tied to one of the wooden uprights, with his ankles and wrists bound tightly, Shaun Tyson was sitting in soiled underwear, drugged and silent, with his forehead resting against the wood.

Sergio received a similar treatment. He was stripped to his underwear and bound to the upright beam, unconscious with his head hanging back, his mouth wide open and his ruined leg at an unnatural angle with a riot of deathly colour forming across the skin.

In front of the two men and the upright beams to which they were bound, an antique copper bathtub with grotesque, gothic, clawed feet and a rolled edge took centre stage.

Beneath it, Harvey had placed a row of powerful gas burners, turned on to their maximum with bright blue flames heating the shiny, copper surface. The water inside that was filled to the brim was beginning to steam. A single light bulb shone a dome of dim, yellow light over the tub as if the main act waited in silence for the unwilling audience to arrive.

The first bubble burst on the steaming surface of the water.

A pair of eyes opened.

Harvey smiled the rare smile of a man whose dreams had come true.

CHAPTER THIRTY-EIGHT

"Carver."

Frank held his desk phone to his ear and stared up at the image of Julios Saville. It was one of two new photos added to his pinboard.

"Sir, you've been requested to join the chief in conference room two," said the secretary.

"I'll be right there. Thank you."

Frank sat back in his chair, took a deep breath, and thought about his wife whose framed photo stared lovingly at him from the desk. She would have been proud. She had always supported him even though she hadn't understood the ins and outs of his work. But she had always been there for him to vent.

She had always been there to cheer him up during those tricky times when Thomson's games had him caught in a web of lies.

He pulled on his jacket, checked his shoes were clean and made his way to the elevator. Nerves whisked his thoughts into a jumbled mix of memories and possibilities. He stared at the digital readout on the elevator, barely noticing the stares, smiles and admiration from colleagues who'd all heard the news.

In the conference room, the chief stood at the head of the room dressed in an expensive, tailored suit, white shirt and gleaming shoes. Melody Mills, Reg Tenant and Denver Cox all sat on one side of the table. Mills was sitting ramrod straight with her notepad, pen and smartphone arranged neatly. Tenant slouched in his seat, his head buried in his phone. Cox picked at the sole of his boot.

"Frank, come in," said the chief.

His boss stepped towards him and offered his hand. Frank shook it then selected a seat opposite his team.

"Thank you all for coming," began the chief. "This won't take long. I know you are all as busy as I am. I'd like to thank you all for your recent efforts. As you are all aware, we've managed to close several unsolved crimes, most of which, thanks to your diligence, were the result of finding Julios Saville. It would have been a real pleasure to bring him in with a pulse. But, beggars can't be choosers. By good police work or good fortune, you've managed to close more unsolved organised crime cases in the past day than we have in the past six months."

While the chief took a sip of water, Frank's team glanced at each other with pride.

"Next up," continued the chief, "not only did you bring in one of the most wanted men in Britain, but you also managed to find twelve missing Heckler and Koch MP5s. If I'm honest, they shouldn't have been missing at all. They were British service weapons, and all eyes were on them. So well done. Bloody good show."

Mills, Tenant and Cox smiled at the thanks from the chief. Frank stared at the wall, avoiding eye contact.

"Lastly," said the chief, "we have the case of one Mr Terry Thomson. I don't need to go into his record, but needless to say, the man was a menace and had evaded prison for far too long. I can't credit his death to you, Frank, but your actions have caused the downfall of this murderous family and consequently made our streets a safer place. Damn fine work."

"I couldn't have done it without my team," said Frank.

"There's no room here for modesty, Frank," said the chief. "You did a damn good job, all of you."

Beneath the shining appraisal, a pang of sickening guilt began to turn inside Frank's stomach. Another lie to cover a lie. Thomson's final stab reached out from the grave and cut the pleasure Frank so deserved.

"So, here's what I'd like to do," said the chief. "I have a proposition for you."

"For me, sir?" said Frank.

"No, Frank. For all of you. You see, while the force continues to increase resources in counter-terrorism, there's been a rise in domestic organised crime."

"Gangs, sir?" asked Mills.

"That's right. While the country fights a war against terrorism, these criminals are taking liberties. It's like the eighties all over again. You remember the eighties, Frank?"

"The best days of my career, sir," said Frank with a weak smile.

"Good. Because if you play your cards right, you'll be running a domestic, covert special ops unit whose sole focus is to combat organised crime in London. How does that sound?"

"And my team?" asked Frank.

"You can have the pick of the bunch, Frank. Anyone out there, you name them, and I'll make it happen."

"Anyone?"

"Pretty much. Within reason," said the chief.

"What about resources?" asked Frank.

"You'll build a report with a budget. Be gentle, of course. We can see about getting you more next year. Tell me what your team would look like."

"Well, I'll need someone smart," said Frank, his eyes fixed on Mills. "Someone dependable, brave, intelligent, and who can shoot the arse off a fly at a thousand yards."

"Good," said the chief. "I've got just the person in mind. Who else?"

"I'll need tech research. In fact, I'll need

the finest techie the force can offer," said Frank, looking at Tenant.

"I'm sure that can be arranged," replied the chief, making a note on his pad.

"Anything else?"

"Logistics," said Frank. His eyes moved to Cox. "I'll need a world-class driver and one of the best helicopter pilots we have."

"That's a push, Frank," replied the chief. "I can get you the driver, but a pilot would be well above your budget."

"You don't understand, sir," said Frank, smiling at the three individuals who stared back at him, red-faced but beaming with pride. "I have my team right here."

CHAPTER THIRTY-NINE

Sucking in air through gritted teeth, Sergio reeled with pain and reached for his leg with his bound hands, but failed.

"Harvey," said Sergio between rasping gasps. "Harvey, untie me now. Why are you doing this?"

But his efforts at authority faded as his voice fell to a child-like sob. It reminded Harvey of a time when, as a child, he had crept into the kitchen in the early hours, drawn by the whimpering of innocence. He remembered the screams with audible clarity. He felt the bite of the cold, tiled floor on his young, bare feet. He remembered how he'd dared not move as a figure emerged from the basement, satiated, as the crying and whimpering started over with renewed vigour.

"I saw them, Sergio," said Harvey. "Your eyes."

"What? What are you talking about? Let me go, damn it."

"I saw them at her funeral. You were *shamed*, not sad. It all makes sense now."

"Whose funeral, Harvey? Just tell me what you want."

"You remember her, don't you? Hannah?"

Sergio didn't reply.

"Ah, I thought so. You remember her *well*."

"I don't know what you're talking about, Harvey. Of course, I remember her. She was your sister."

"But you remember her better than most, don't you? Not *Jack* of course. He remembered her as well as you do. But he doesn't remember her anymore. He doesn't remember anything, does he? You do remember Jack, don't you, Sergio?"

"Harvey, I don't know what you want from me. But tell me. You can have it. Please, Harvey."

Sergio was fighting for breaths between

sobs. His body convulsed as he cried. It was a scene Harvey had seen more than a dozen times when the guilty face justice and retribution.

"*Please*, Harvey. All these years I've taken care of you."

"All these years, Sergio, you've lied to me."

"What? Tell me what you want. You can have anything."

"There's nothing you can volunteer, Sergio. The only thing I want is your suffering."

"I *am* suffering, Harvey. Look at me. I'll never walk again."

"You'll never do many things again," snapped Harvey. Then he checked his emotions as Julios had always instructed. "You're going to die a very painful death, Sergio."

Harvey strolled to the tub and felt the water temperature with his finger. The water was warming. Not hot yet. But not cold.

In a rush of panic, Shaun came to consciousness. Finding himself restrained and semi-naked, he fought his restraints for a few brief moments but soon gave up.

"What the...Where am I? Who are *you*?" he said to Sergio. "What's going on?"

Harvey shot him a glance, and Shaun silenced as recognition set in.

"You woke in time for the show, Shaun. Do you know Sergio?" Harvey presented Sergio with an open palm.

"No, I...I don't think I do. I know *you* though. You're the man-"

"Shh, keep the noise down, Shaun. This is a civilised show. We don't want the cast spoiling it for the audience, do we?"

Shaun searched the shadows. "Where the bloody hell am I?"

"You are both about to suffer for your sins," said Harvey, using his left hand to present the bathtub to the men. "Who's first?"

As expected, neither man spoke.

"Should *I* choose?"

"Harvey, you sick son of a bitch. You can't do this. John won't allow it. Your *father* won't allow it."

"Oh, Sergio, you know me better than that, don't you? Do you honestly think I'd do anything to upset the family business?"

"See, so you can't kill me. I know too much. The business won't run without me."

"I can assure you John has everything he needs to continue without you, Sergio. In fact,

I think he'll be pleased to get rid of you." Harvey paused. "So shall we get started? Seeing as neither of you wants to go first, we'll have a competition."

The two condemned men glanced at each other in confusion.

"Let's start with Shaun. I feel we ought to get to know you a little better. Confess."

"Eh?"

"Confess, Shaun. Do I need to explain the definition of the word confess?"

"No."

"What does it mean then?"

"To own up."

"Good. Now confess."

"To what?"

Harvey didn't reply. Instead, he stood, turned the chair around and straddled it, then leaned forward on the back of the chair with his chin on his arms, ready for the show.

"The more you confess," said Harvey, "the easier I will make it on you. Whoever offers the poorest confession is the loser, and losers bath first. Does that sound fair?"

Once more, the two men exchanged glances.

"Okay, I'll *tell* you," said Sergio.

"No, no, no, Sergio. You had your chance. But don't worry. That was just a warm-up round. You'll get another go soon enough," said Harvey, offering the man a wink and a glare.

"I was young," began Shaun. "I was raped."

"That's not really a confession, Shaun," said Harvey. "That's an excuse."

"I know. But that's when it all started," said Shaun. "Ever since then, I've had these urges."

"Urges?"

Harvey leaned forward with interest.

"Tell me about the first time you had one of your urges, Shaun."

CHAPTER FORTY

"Tell me what you'd need," said the chief.

Pondering the question, Frank, who had never considered such an opportunity, tried to think on his feet. But the truth was, he was overwhelmed. He was unprepared and still reeling from the glowing appraisal that, if the truth came out, would all come crashing down like a house of cards.

"We'd need an HQ, sir," said Mills, sensing Frank's struggle with words. "Somewhere to set up, keep our kit, and run the operations."

"Couldn't you do that from here?" asked the chief.

"Not covert, sir. Plus, you can't do anything here without it being all around the cafeteria by lunchtime."

"Agreed," said Frank. "It doesn't have to be huge, but close to London City Airport for domestic flights, and near to the A13 to access London and the motorway network. Oh, and close to the River Thames."

"In case you decide to ask for a boat next year?" asked the chief with a grin.

"I'll need dual, dark fibre connections to the internet and Metropolitan network, sir," said Tenant. "Plus, unhindered access to satellites and some hardware. I can get you a list. It'll be long but practical."

"Right," said the chief, making notes in his pad. "And what is it you intend on doing with all this, Tenant? Build a supercomputer?"

"Yes, sir. Exactly that," replied Tenant, matter of fact.

Frank shrugged, smiled and glanced across at Denver Cox, inviting him to voice his requests.

"I'll need a workshop," said Cox. "Somewhere I can work on the motors."

"Motors?" said the chief. "Plural?"

"We don't need anything too fancy, sir," replied Cox. "A saloon, fast and sleek for undercover work, an Audi or something. Plus we'll need a new van."

"I thought your team has a van?"

"No, it's beat," said Cox, before Frank could interject. "For an operation like this, we'd need something new. Something a bit more reliable."

"Okay," said the chief, adding the request to his list. "How about you, Mills?"

"I won't need a lot, sir," she replied. "Two Diemaco assault rifles. The C8 is a good option with the underslung grenade launcher. Half a dozen Heckler and Koch MP5s. The seven-point-six-two, if possible. For handguns, we'd need a good number of Sig two-two-eights and two-two-sixes. Plus we'd need an armoury to keep them locked up, fireproof, of course. Then for surveillance, I'd need a few pairs of Steiner binoculars. None of the auto-focus type. I prefer manual focus. A few NV kits would be good. A set of body armour each. Plus listening devices. Standard issue is fine."

The room was silent when she finished; it continued that way while the chief noted her requests as fast as he could write them.

"You gave that a little thought, didn't you, Mills?" he said, eventually.

"It's my dream armoury, sir. Everything a girl needs to keep the boys in their place."

The comment brought a smile to the chief's face.

He announced the meeting's closure with a snap of his notepad.

"So there we have it. But there's one last thing before I go upstairs and put my neck on the line."

"What's that, sir?" said Frank, sensing a curveball.

"You found twelve of the missing MP5s, and for that, I'm very grateful. Believe me, there's only one thing worse than wars being fought on British soil, and that's people being killed with weapons that belong to the British military. You can imagine the position it puts me in."

"We can," said Frank, speaking for the team. "I don't envy your responsibilities."

"No," said the chief. "So before I go and potentially make myself the laughing stock of the force, and before you all get your dream headquarters, you're going to go out there and do whatever it takes to bring those weapons back home."

"You want us to find the other twelve MP5s?" said Frank, more in disbelief than for clarification.

"You find me those weapons, Frank," said the chief, raising his glass of water as if it were a champagne flute, "and I'll get you all your dream jobs."

CHAPTER FORTY-ONE

"Do you feel better for that, Shaun?" asked Harvey, breaking the silence following his confession.

With his legs curled around the beam and his head resting on the smooth oak, shame fell from Shaun's face in little drops. He started to say more as if by vocalising his crimes, somehow everything would be okay.

"Now, now, Shaun," said Harvey. "It's Sergio's turn."

But Sergio just stared at Shaun, horrified at the story he'd heard.

"Come on, Sergio. You had plenty to say a while ago."

"What? What do you want to know?"

Harvey's eyes narrowed.

"What's the worst thing you ever did?"

"I've never killed anybody."

Harvey stared, impassive.

"I set fire to a dog once?"

Harvey didn't reply.

"I was just a kid."

"Stop there, Sergio. Did you hear what Shaun just told us? Did you hear the shame in his voice? The conviction in his voice?"

The silence was broken by Shaun shuffling around the beam, seeking comfort on the cold, hard floor and a better view of Sergio, whose confession was imminent.

"Jack found her," said Sergio. Then he paused.

"And I found *Jack*, didn't I?" said Harvey.

"He went first," said Sergio.

"*Sergio*, come on. Tell me a story. I want the details. How did she get down here?"

"She was getting a drink of water. It was late or early. Nighttime." Sergio closed his eyes, reliving the night for the thousandth time in his tortured mind. "We'd been playing cards in John's study. We were gambling and drinking. We heard someone on the stairs outside. The last step always creaked."

"It still does," said Harvey.

"We heard her footsteps. They were loud in the quiet night. So Jack got up and looked around the door to make sure it wasn't John's wife."

"My foster mother?"

"Yes. Barb. She didn't approve of our gambling in the house. But Jack grew excited, waving us over from the door. We stepped out into the hallway like naughty children, giggling and whispering. She was wearing a nightshirt with little panties, and well..."

"Well? Well, what?"

It was sorrow rather than shame that Harvey saw in his eyes. The shame came after the fact. It always did.

"She was a half-naked young woman, and she was...beautiful."

"She *was* beautiful, Sergio."

"Jack led us into the kitchen. We followed like sheep. I sensed something was wrong. It all felt wrong. He crept up behind her and grabbed her by the waist to surprise her. But she fought him off. Although he was only playing, she resisted. He kept going, tickling her and squeezing her."

Never before had Harvey heard the

words of another man with such clarity. It was the one story he'd never wanted to hear, but it was the one story he had needed to hear since he'd been a small boy, since the night that had changed his life.

"He took it too far and felt her chest. So she slapped him. Hard. He slapped her back harder, and she fell down, hitting her head on the tiled floor. But something came over Jack. He was different, almost enchanted. He bent down beside her, running his hand along her leg and..."

"And, Sergio?" said Harvey, imagining the scene with sickened distaste, forcing himself to endure what Hannah had endured, to understand the root of the misery that killed her.

"He *touched* her," said Sergio, closing his eyes once more and reliving the nightmare.

He was in the dream, as was Harvey.

"He called us over. 'Sergio, get the door,' he whispered to me. Then he lifted her so her long hair hung from his arms, and he carried her down the steps to this place."

Sergio nodded his head to the steps.

"He laid her on the bench that was there and stripped her naked like some kind of wild animal, tearing at her nightshirt. He was overcome with awe. There was no talking to him. We tried, but he just kept touching her, feeling her smooth skin against his rough hands. He was taken by her, Harvey. He always had been."

It was Shaun's turn to stare aghast at the story. He sat with his mouth wide open, listening with horror at the events that had destroyed Harvey's family. Harvey noticed him, the expression on his face and compassion in his eyes.

"He was on top of her when she woke," continued Sergio. "She tried to fight him, of course. But he was a strong man, too strong for a girl. But still, she fought until Jack hit her and she passed out again. The next time she woke, all her courage and strength had been taken. She just lay there crying and letting him..."

"And when he finished?"

"Jack left," said Sergio, nodding once more at the steps.

"And you?"

Sergio looked up at Harvey. His mouth was turned down in an arc of disgrace and shame.

He nodded. "Yes," he whispered.

"Yes?" said Harvey, feeling the familiar touch of a talon in the pit of his stomach.

"I raped her."

A stab of the beast added finality to the words Harvey had been waiting for his whole life.

"Tell me, Sergio," said Harvey, feeling the release of adrenaline into his body and the racing pulse of his heart flash behind his eyes. "Tell me what you did."

"I hit her again. I knocked her unconscious," said Sergio. Then he paused, but he'd gone too far to stop. "I raped her. Your sister. It was me. The man you've been looking for. I'm so sorry, Harvey. I'm so sorry."

Once more, the room was filled with the whining sobs of shame, guilt, and as Harvey stood from the chair, fear.

"I think we have a *winner*," he said.

An audible sigh escaped Shaun's lips, but he watched with horrified joy as Harvey untied Sergio's bindings.

"You're letting me go?"

For a brief moment, a flash of hope showed itself across the lines on Sergio's gaunt face.

But Harvey was only just beginning. He

took slow steps to the corner of the room, savouring the waking beast's sharp claws and the tingle in his limbs. Fetching a coil of rope, he cast one end over a high horizontal beam and then tested the temperature of the bubbling water.

"I think we're ready," said Harvey, allowing a thick wave of steam to engulf his face in the dim light.

With a practised hand, Harvey tied one end of the rope to Sergio's wrists, finishing the knot with a sharp snatch. Then, like a curious child might follow a trail of sweets, Harvey traced the rope's length to the bath, and up and over the beam where he found the loose end.

He pulled once, taking the slack and snatching Sergio to one side.

"Don't do this, Harvey. I told you what you wanted to hear."

Harvey pulled again and again, feeding off Sergio's wild complaints, until Sergio's feet rose above the bath and steam engulfed him, teasing him with the flavour of heat below.

"Are you watching, Shaun?" said Harvey.

"Yes, sir," said Shaun, transfixed by the sheer terror of the scene.

"I want you to watch, Shaun. I want you to think about what he did," said Harvey, tying the rope off to the clawed foot of the bathtub. "Are you thinking, Shaun?"

"Yes, sir."

"What are you thinking?"

"About what he said he did."

"No, Harvey. Stop. Please," said Sergio.

"Tell me what he did, Shaun," said Harvey, overpowering Sergio's feeble pleas for mercy.

"He raped your sister," said Shaun, as if by uttering the words, he cast guilt upon himself.

"Do you know what she did *after*, Shaun?"

"Harvey, stop."

"No, sir."

"Harvey, *stop* this. It's stupid," Sergio begged.

"Tell Shaun what Hannah did after you raped her, Sergio."

"Harvey, come on. It's hot. This is not a game."

"Tell him, Sergio," said Harvey, his voice a whisper in the steam.

"She killed herself. Is that what you want

to hear?"

"But what did she do, Sergio?"

"She cut herself. Let me go, Harvey. I'm slipping."

"She cut herself, Shaun. Sergio, tell Shaun where she cut herself."

"Ahh, Harvey. *No.* Stop. My foot, it's burning," cried Sergio, as his hands slipped further through the knot, wet with the condensed steam on his skin.

"Tell him, Sergio. You remember, don't you? Of course you do."

"*Everywhere,*" Sergio shouted. "Everywhere we'd been. She cut herself to ribbons. Now let me go, Harvey. Please."

"I'll put an end to it soon, Sergio."

A jolt, as the rope eased further along Sergio's hands, stopped at his purple knuckles. But unable to raise his ruined leg, his foot submerged in the frantic water. The room filled with a fresh scream, louder than before.

"I need one more answer, Sergio. Then it's bath time."

"What? Tell me what you what to know. Just let me go."

"You said *we.*"

"What?" replied Sergio. "When?"

"In the study, Sergio. It was quite clear. Jack called *us* over."

Sergio slipped lower. His entire foot stirred in the boiling water, turning an angry red, and blistering with almost immediate effect.

"It was a mistake, Harvey. I was scared. I don't know what I was-"

"If you tell me, Sergio, I'll end it now," said Harvey, his cold tone cutting through the heat of the boiling steam. "Who was the third man?"

Sergio didn't reply.

"I can end this now, Sergio. Or I can make it a whole lot worse for you," said Harvey, drawing his knife from the sheath on his belt. He ran it across Sergio's groin, which hung at head height. "Tell me who it was."

"Ah, I *can't*," sobbed Sergio.

With a flick of his wrist, Harvey turned the blade, digging the sharp point at the bulge between Sergio's legs. He jabbed up lightly but hard enough to remind Sergio of his predicament.

"Ah, *no*."

"Sergio."

"No."

"*Tell me.*"

"I can't."

"Sergio."

He pushed the knife harder.

"*Donny*. It was Donny. He was the third man. He went after me. It was his first time."

The words came at Harvey like a blow to his gut. He stepped back, dizzied, dropping the knife to his side, and sucking in a lungful of hot steamy air.

"Thank you, Sergio."

Then Harvey paused to take one last look at Hannah's killer.

"Thank you."

He'd imagined the moment a thousand times.

But now his imagination was completed. The faceless man that had suffered at Harvey's hands in so many dreams was now real. He could reach out and touch him, hurt him, feed off his fear.

Instead, he swiped once with the knife. The blade slashed through the manila rope with ease. Peace fell over Harvey as Sergio, who moments before had begged for life with wretched cries, writhed and struggled in the searing, angry water, begging for death.

CHAPTER FORTY-TWO

Loud sobbing and whimpering like that of a child sang out from somewhere far away as if a tortured soul was constrained to the house for eternity, existing in the old walls and shadows and feeding off the lifeless air.

To the right and left of the two huge front doors were two rooms equal in size. The first was an office with a large desk, matching bookshelves and a drinks cabinet, on top of which was a silver platter containing a crystal decanter and two upturned crystal tumblers. One held traces of amber liquid in the bottom. Lowering his face to the glass, Frank inhaled the rich scent of brandy, teasing himself.

Then he stood, his eye-catching a single bullet mark almost concealed within the pattern of the flock wallpaper.

Instinct popped open the strap that secured his weapon in the holster beneath his arm. But he did not remove the gun. He preferred to take in the feel of the building. Still, the cries came like the waves of an ocean, whispered and tantalising.

The adjacent room held little interest. It had a dining table, rarely used judging by the dust, and couches that might have come from the set of an eighties television show. What once might've been the scene of opulent dinner parties had faded to near ruin. A snapshot in time.

A large double staircase was the central feature of the grand hallway. It curved like two snakes ready to strike those who dared pass between.

Frank dared.

To the rear of the house, a large kitchen with terracotta tiles seemed to be the only room graced by sunlight. Large windows ran from left to right, old-fashioned pots and pans hung from oak beams, and to Frank's right was a doorway. It stood open a few inches, releasing the cries of the tortured soul. A part of the house itself.

Frank stepped inside.

Below, at the foot of a set of hard, concrete steps, a dim light shone across a floor of bare concrete and a thick, acrid smell of death and human waste tainted the air Frank breathed.

With each step, the dim light revealed more.

Two hideous cast iron feet.

The sobbing had stopped as if Frank's presence had been sensed.

A copper bathtub, an antique, its sides gleaming and its top edge finished with a marvellous roll by the skilled hand of a smith a century before.

A human arm, swollen and white with death, the skin melted and stuck to the side of the bath like candle wax.

With slow, quiet movements, Frank unholstered his weapon and stepped onto the concrete floor. Staring back at him, with eyes boiled white and skin seared, a boiled man lay partly submerged and motionless.

"He's dead."

The voice from the corner of the room startled Frank, who raised his weapon with shaky hands, aiming at the source of the voice.

"Don't shoot. Don't shoot," said the boy, who cowered behind the single oak upright beam he hugged.

Checking the shadowed corners of the room with renewed fear, Frank returned to the boy, who watched his every move and held the wooden upright as if he would never let go.

"What's your name?" asked Frank. "What *happened* here?"

The boy didn't reply.

Only when Frank stepped closer, eyeing the boy's stained underwear, did he see the bindings on his wrists and ankles. Two eyes stared up at Frank. But they weren't the pleading eyes of a captive. Nor were they the harrowed eyes of a survivor. They were the eyes of the shamed, riddled with guilt.

A single object caught Frank's eye, out of place in the room where it seemed time stood still. On an old cabinet that had been covered with a dust sheet was an audio recorder sitting on top of a folded note.

He glanced back at the boy and then to the bath. Death stared across the room. He followed the gaze and found a small tape recorder. Frank pushed the play button and the tiny tape kicked into life. The background noise was hissy and busy. There were no voices. Just the sound, Frank assumed, of boiling water.

"What's the worst thing you ever did?" said a man's voice.

Frank hit stop as footsteps behind him on the stairs grew closer. He turned, aimed, and came face to face with Mills, who lowered her weapon and sighed with relief.

"Sir?"

"Mills," replied Frank, lowering his gun. "How did you find me?"

"Tenant, sir," said Mills. "What happened here?"

"That's exactly what I'm piecing together."

"You found Shaun Tyson?" said Mills, nodding at the boy. "How does he fit into all this?"

"You know him?" asked Frank.

"Sex offender, sir. Skipped bail earlier this week."

"Call uniforms to take him away and get the boy a blanket or something," said Frank.

As Frank and Mills walked through the two huge front doors and into the grounds of the house, savouring the sweet smell of fresh air, three police cars sped through the gates, skidding to a halt in the gravel. The rhythmic thudding of an approaching helicopter killed any remaining peace as the uniforms approached the front doors. Flashing her ID, Mills pointed to the kitchen.

"Basement," she said, then returned her attention to Frank. "Well, a sex offender wasn't quite what I was wishing for, sir. But it's still a win."

"Follow me," said Frank.

With his hands in the deep pockets of his overcoat, Frank strolled away from the house and onto the wide expanse of lawn to a large single-story building with a row of three double garage doors at the front. The last one was open as if inviting them inside. Approaching with caution and with their weapons raised, the two scanned the interior. Frank walked along the front of the car collection and Mills took the rear.

"There's no-one here, sir," said Mills.

"No," replied Frank. "I didn't expect there to be. He's long gone."

"So what's the significance?"

Between an immaculate E-Type Jaguar and an old Triumph Spitfire was a white van.

"I found a note," said Frank. "In the basement."

"From him?" asked Mills.

Frank nodded.

"What did it say?" asked Mills, as a child might pester a parent.

"Two words," said Frank. "A gift."

"A gift? Is that all?"

"So Shaun Tyson was a gift?"

"No. Shaun Tyson is a lucky boy. He'll serve time, for sure. But my guess is that whoever that is in the bath was the cause of our man's issues."

Mills considered Frank's words then summarised.

"So he no longer needed Tyson? He found what he'd been looking for?"

"That's what I think," said Frank, stopping his slow pace at the rear of the van.

"So what was the gift?" asked Mills. "The dead guy?"

But Frank just shook his head.

"Are you ready for this?" he asked.

"Ready for what, sir?" she asked.

With a smile that conveyed the end of a journey and so much more to come, Frank gestured at the van.

"Open the doors."

CHAPTER FORTY-THREE

Tall, wild grass edged a fine beach of golden sand. Long, finger-like clouds stretched from the horizon across the expanse of blue sky. The rushing tide of the sea crashed forward, dispersed, then retreated back to join the ranks. At the edge of the beach near the long grass, Harvey Stone lay in the sand, feeling the warmth of the French sun on his face.

In his hands was an English newspaper. It was several days old. The headline story reported a diamond heist in the north of England that detectives were investigating. No shots had been fired. No blood had been spilt. No sign had been found that the robbery had even taken place, save for a tunnel that had been concealed by a large painting, revealed only by a few crumbs of broken concrete.

Investigators estimated that the thieves had been tunnelling for at least three weeks in advance of the diamonds' arrival in Manchester, where the gems were being held overnight. The plan had been carried out with meticulous perfection. Once more, a rare and beautiful smile crept over Harvey's face, as he lay back, thought of Stimson with the diamonds, and felt the sun wash across his eyelids.

Dreams of a small boy chasing his sister through the long, wild grasses at the edge of a beach came to him. This time, the boy caught her, and they rolled, laughing as children do.

The sunshine on Harvey's eyelids fell into shadow. The temperature dropped a degree or two and a presence woke him.

"You're in the light," said Harvey.

"I *am* the light, Mr Stone."

Had the words been uttered at any other time in his life, Harvey may have felt the threat. But he sensed a confident smile in the man's tone.

"Would you mind shining somewhere else then?"

"You're not an easy man to track down."

"I'm not exactly hiding."

"I followed you from Essex."

"I'm not exactly running either," said Harvey, countering the man's statements, waiting for the bite.

"Thanks for the gift," said the man. "But why?"

"I'm done with it all," said Harvey. "It's finished."

"Is that why you spared Tyson?"

"It was never about him. Or the others."

"So you're *finished*, are you?"

"I am."

"It's a shame. You're an interesting man, Mr Stone."

Footsteps in the soft sand preceded the return of the warm sun on Harvey's face.

In his mind's eye, Harvey pictured a man, mid-to-late fifties with grey hair and a paunch. The man had turned to face the sea. It was an invitation for Harvey to run. But concealed in the stranger's confident tone was an underlying message that he would find him wherever Harvey ran.

"How do you want to do this?" the man called, raising his voice above the crashing waves and cool breeze. Soft remnants of a Scottish accent hung at the end of his words.

Rolling onto his side, propped up by an elbow, Harvey opened his eyes and found the man, silhouetted against the sky, his long overcoat flapping in the breeze. Harvey plucked a blade of long grass from the sand and rolled it between his fingers, pondering the words.

"There's another way, you know," said the man. "It doesn't have to end the way you imagine."

"It has ended," replied Harvey, "exactly how I imagined it would."

"I need someone," continued the man.

He turned to stare down at Harvey, faceless with the sun behind him.

"Someone who isn't afraid to get his hands dirty. Somebody with a very particular skill set."

Harvey didn't reply.

The End

Also by J.D. Weston

Award-winning author and creator of Harvey Stone and Frankie Black, J.D.Weston was born in London, England, and after more than a decade in the Middle East, now enjoys a tranquil life in Lincolnshire with his wife.

The Harvey Stone series is the prequel series set ten years before The Stone Cold Thriller series.

With more than twenty novels to J.D. Weston's name, the Harvey Stone series is the result of many years of storytelling, and is his finest work to date. You can find more about J.D. Weston at www.jdweston.com.

Turn the page to see his other books.

The Silent Man

To find the killer, he must lose his mind...

See www.jdweston.com for details.

The Spider's Web

To catch the killer, he must become the fly...

See www.jdweston.com for details.

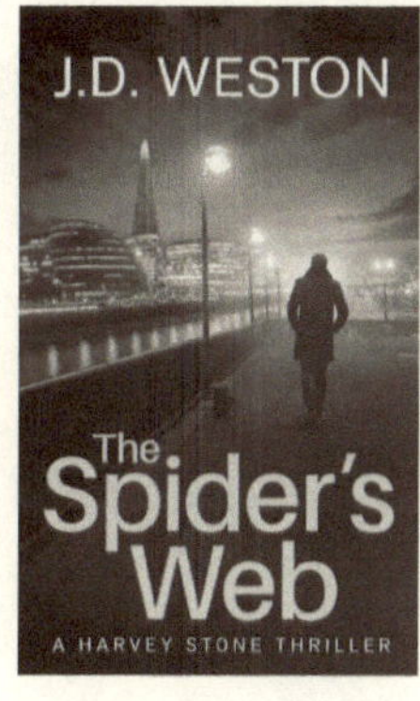

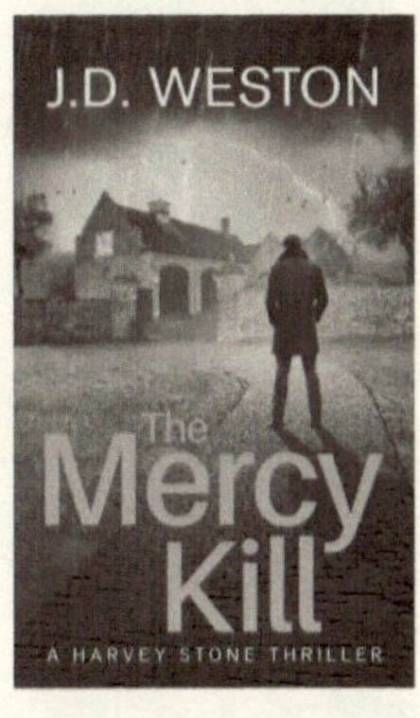

The Mercy Kill

To light the way, he must burn his past...

See www.jdweston.com for details.

The Savage Few

Coming 2021

Join the J.D. Weston Reader Group to stay up to date on new releases, receive discounts, and get three free eBooks.

See www.jdweston.com for details.

THE STONE COLD THRILLER SERIES

The Stone Cold Thriller Series

Stone Cold

Stone Fury

Stone Fall

Stone Rage

Stone Free

Stone Rush

Stone Game

Stone Raid

Stone Deep

Stone Fist

Stone Army

Stone Face

The Stone Cold Box Sets

Boxset One

Boxset Two

Boxset Three

Boxset Four

Visit www.jdweston.com for details.

The Frankie Black Files

Torn in Two

Her Only Hope

Black Blood

The Frankie Black Files Boxset

Visit www.jdweston.com for details.

ACKNOWLEDGEMENTS

Authors are often portrayed as having very lonely work lives. There breeds a stereotypical image of reclusive authors talking only to their cat or dog and their editor, and living off cereal and brandy.

I beg to differ.

There is absolutely no way on the planet that this book could have been created to the standard it is without the help and support of Erica Bawden, Paul Weston, Danny Maguire, and Heather Draper. All of whom offered vital feedback during various drafts and supported me while I locked myself away and spoke to my imaginary dog, ate cereal and drank brandy.

The book was painstakingly edited by Ceri Savage, who continues to sit with me on Skype every week as we flesh out the series, and also throws in some amazing ideas.

To those named above, I am truly grateful.

J.D.Weston.

www.ingramcontent.com/pod-product-compliance
Lightning Source LLC
Chambersburg PA
CBHW060754190726
48285CB00002B/428